DERWENT VALE PRIMARY

DERWENT VALE PRIMARY

KING-SMITH, D.

Find the white horse

CUMBRIA COUNTY LIBRARY

This book is due for return on or before the last date above. It may be renewed by personal application, post or telephone, if not in demand.

C.L.18

KT-491-300

Some other books by Dick King-Smith

DICK KING-SMITH

—FIND THE—
WHITE HORSE

Illustrated by Larry Wilkes

CUMBRIA COUNTY ASK LIBRARY

PUFFIN BOOKS

PUFFIN BOOKS

Published by the Penguin Group
Penguin Books Ltd, 27 Wrights Lane, London W8 5TZ, England
Penguin Books USA Inc., 375 Hudson Street, New York, New York 10014, USA
Penguin Books Australia Ltd, Ringwood, Victoria, Australia
Penguin Books Canada Ltd, 10 Alcorn Avenue, Toronto, Ontario, Canada M4V 3B2
Penguin Books (NZ) Ltd, 182–190 Wairau Road, Auckland 10, New Zealand

Penguin Books Ltd, Registered Offices: Harmondsworth, Middlesex, England

First published by Viking 1991
Published in Puffin Books 1993
5 7 9 10 8 6 4

Text copyright © Fox Busters Limited, 1991
Illustrations copyright © Larry Wilkes, 1991
All rights reserved

The moral right of the author has been asserted

Filmset in Century Schoolbook

Made and printed in England by Clays Ltd, St Ives plc

Except in the United States of America, this book is sold subject
to the condition that it shall not, by way of trade or otherwise, be lent,
re-sold, hired out, or otherwise circulated without the publisher's
prior consent in any form of binding or cover other than that in
which it is published and without a similar condition including this
condition being imposed on the subsequent purchaser

Contents

Chapter One

IN THE NICK
OF TIME

They say that people often look very like the animals that they keep. That would have been difficult for the Manager of the Dogs' Home, for in it, at any one time, were always lots of very different-looking dogs, so that he could not possibly have resembled them all.

In fact, the Manager had a rather sharp face with a pointed chin, and a whiskery little moustache and small neat ears, so that he looked much more like a cat than a dog. Which was odd, because he hated cats.

In particular he hated the one and only cat that lived at the Dogs' Home. It was a Siamese tom, belonging to the Manager's wife.

She had bought it as a kitten, and had made a great fuss of it for a while, and then – for she was that sort of a person – had grown bored with it and paid it no attention.

The only attention it got was from the Manager, in the shape of a sly kick aimed at it whenever they met. The Manager nursed a secret hope that the cat would find its way

into the kennel of a large fierce dog.

In the central part of the Dogs' Home was the kennel-block, a row of a dozen wired enclosures facing a similar row, with a corridor in between. Every morning the cat came down the corridor on a tour of inspection of whatever stray or lost or unwanted dogs chanced to be in the Home at that time.

He came chiefly out of a sense of mischief. It was fun to rub himself against the wire of the kennel doors and listen to the furious growls and barks and yaps and snarls of the inmates, inches away, as they told him in no uncertain terms just what they would do with him if only they could get at him.

Not all of them did this – some were too

dispirited to take notice of him – but certainly no dog had ever said a kind word to him. Until one day he made a friend.

There was a new arrival that morning, a large and hairy mongrel whose collar carried a metal disc that said simply LUBBER. His ears were floppy, his tail was long and bushy, and in colour he was white with brown patches. The Siamese was on his rounds at the time, and he waited until the kennelmaid had shut the dog in and gone away. Then he rubbed himself against the wire and waited for the outburst. None came. Instead the big mongrel looked down at the cat and wagged his tail, with a kind of grin on his hairy face.

'Hello,' he said. 'I'm Lubber. What do they call you?'

'Squintum,' said the Siamese.

Slender and elegant, with a short glossy coat and eyes of a brilliant blue, he was a very well-bred cat, but with a fault. Siamese should actually not be the least bit cross-eyed. Squintum was.

'Well, it's jolly nice to meet you!' said Lubber in his deep voice. 'And I shall look forward to having a good old chinwag later. But just now, I'm tired out. Do forgive me, I simply can't keep my eyes open,' and he lay down upon the bench at the back of the kennel, and fell fast asleep.

Cats are nothing if not curious, and in the days that followed, Squintum spent a good deal of time outside Lubber's kennel. There was not much in the way of conversation between them for it was plain that Lubber, as well as being large and clumsy-looking, was the laziest of dogs, and each morning he would excuse himself after a few words and go back to sleep. But those few words were always kindly and friendly ones, and Squintum had never before been treated in such a way by a dog.

Accordingly, as time passed, he grew worried for his new friend, because he knew the rules of the Dogs' Home. Every morning, round about eleven o'clock, any dog that had not been claimed or placed after two weeks in

the Home was taken from its kennel to the vet's surgery along the corridor. There it was painlessly destroyed.

On the thirteenth morning of Lubber's confinement, when the clock on the wall of the kennel-block said five minutes to eleven, a kennelmaid came in. She opened the door of one of the kennels and took away a small, jolly-looking black-and-white terrier, not much more than a pup.

'Where are they going?' asked Lubber.

'For a little walk,' said Squintum shortly.

That night he made his way out into the streets of the town, and sat on a wall in the moonlight, and looked back at the shadowy outline of the Dogs' Home, and thought about freedom.

I can go where I please, he thought, and

some, a few, of those dogs in there may come out of that prison, but for Lubber, tomorrow, it will be too late. Unless I can help. Worth a try, surely?

And so, next morning, Squintum sat waiting and watching, his long thin tail curled neatly round him, as the kennelmaid opened Lubber's door. Lubber, of course, was asleep. Five minutes more, thought Squintum, and you will sleep for ever.

'Come on, old chap!' said the kennelmaid brightly. 'We're going for a little walk,' and as the big dog got to his feet, yawning, she fastened a lead on to his collar.

'What a shame!' she said, stroking the hairy head. 'Can't think why someone hasn't claimed you. Or why someone didn't want you for a pet. Must have been because you're such a lazy old

thing, I think. Every time anybody came to choose a dog, you were asleep. They probably thought you were ill. Ah well! Come along then, Lubber. At least you won't feel anything.'

She led Lubber out and along the corridor. Squintum followed. It was three minutes to eleven.

In the surgery, the vet was loading a syringe. He turned as the door opened and the kennelmaid and the dog came in. Unobserved, Squintum slipped through behind them.

The vet looked consideringly at Lubber.

'He's a big one,' he said, laying down the syringe. 'Don't try to lift him up on to the table by yourself, you'll slip a disc. I'll give you a hand. Does he need muzzling?'

'No,' said the kennelmaid. 'He wouldn't bite anyone. It'd be too much effort. He's ever such a lazy old thing.'

Together they lifted Lubber up on to the table, where he stood patiently, wagging his tail, slowly, so as not to tire himself, and gave them a smily look from under his bushy eyebrows.

The vet picked up a pair of scissors.

'Just going to take a little of this hair off your foreleg, old fellow,' he said, and he snipped away, making a small, close-cropped patch. Then he felt for a vein.

'Right,' said the vet, 'that'll do,' and to the kennelmaid he said, 'Just grip the leg tight, here,' and he picked up the syringe. With his other hand he patted Lubber, who wagged a trifle faster.

'Now,' said the vet, 'this won't hurt.'

Through the surgery window came the sound of a distant church clock, striking the first stroke of eleven.

Siamese have particularly harsh voices, unpleasant to many people's ears, and just as the vet was about to slip the needle into the vein, Squintum let out a sudden ear-splitting yowl.

To the two startled humans the noise, of course, meant nothing. It was just a nuisance and a distraction, making the vet put down his syringe and the kennelmaid release her hold on the dog's leg.

But to Lubber, wondering why he was being made to stand on a table and feeling he would be much more comfortable lying down and perhaps taking a nap, it was clear what the Siamese was saying.

'Run for it!' squalled Squintum at the top of his awful voice. 'Follow me! Or else they'll kill you!'

Chapter Two

OUT THROUGH
THE DOOR

Lubber was not the most quick-witted of dogs,
and the full meaning of Squintum's final
words hadn't really dawned upon him. But he
had been trained, from a puppy, to respond to
simple commands, and now he had received
two – to run for it and to follow the cat – and
he obeyed. With one mighty leap, he was off
the table and out of the surgery door. Behind
him, the vet and the kennelmaid stood open-
mouthed. On the floor, knocked off by a passing blow from Lubber's shaven foreleg, lay
the syringe.

Along the corridor raced Squintum, and
into the kennel-block. Unlike the inmates of
the Dogs' Home, who knew only their prison
cells, Squintum knew every inch of the place.

Now, like all their kind, the dogs in the
kennel-block grew wildly excited as Squintum
sped down the central passage between their
cages, followed, at his best speed, by the lum-
bering Lubber. Here was a scene to relieve
the monotony of their days! How each and

15

every one of them longed to be in Lubber's place, doing what all right-minded dogs should do – chase a cat!

'Go get him, Lubber boy!' they shouted. 'Knock his block off! Beat the living daylights out of him! Tear 'im and eat 'im!'

On ran the Siamese, the bloodthirsty cries dying away behind him, through the office, through the Manager's sitting-room, through the kitchen, making for the back door. Behind him Lubber galloped wildly, swerving round corners, sliding on polished floors, skidding on rugs, knocking over little tables bearing little ornaments that broke into little pieces, intent only on following the cat as he had been told.

Squintum was the most quick-witted of cats, but on this occasion not quick enough. Intent only on saving the dog's life, he had moment-arily forgotten the difference in their sizes.

The back door of the Dogs' Home was a

glass-panelled one, with a metal cat-flap set in the bottom of it, through which went Squintum with the ease of long practice and the speed of light. Passers-by in the street outside saw a lean cream-coloured cat with a dark face and legs and tail come shooting out of a cat-flap, and then they jumped in startled surprise.

With a shattering crash, the glass-panelled back door of the Dogs' Home exploded into a thousand shards and splinters, as through it, as easily as if it had been a paper hoop in a circus ring, burst a large hairy dog. Away he went in pursuit of the distant cat, and then there was nothing to be heard but a tiny tinkling as a last fragment of glass fell on to the pavement.

Squintum was making for the park, by a short cut, through quiet back streets. Lubber, it was plain, was accident-prone, and the Siamese saw little point in saving a life only to have it extinguished beneath the wheels of a passing car or lorry. Also, he wanted to confuse possible pursuers, so he doubled and twisted through a maze of narrow alleys and passageways until he came to the park gates.

Over the grass he ran, past the ornamental gardens and the adventure playground, till he came to the bandstand, in the centre of the park. Up its steps he went, and stopped in the middle of its circular interior, and sat and waited.

In a minute or two Lubber arrived, puffing and blowing like a grampus, and flumped down upon the ground, exhausted. Squintum waited for the big dog to get his breath back.

He speculated upon Lubber's probable first words. After all, he thought, I've just saved his life.

'Oh, how can I ever thank you enough?'

That's what he'll probably say.

But then he heard a snore.

'Lubber!' said Squintum sharply. 'I hope you realize that I've just saved your life?'

Lubber sat up. It is not possible to say that he looked shamefaced, for his face was so hairy as to be expressionless. But he scratched himself in an embarrassed way, and seemed unwilling to meet the slightly in-turned gaze of the Siamese's blue eyes.

'I don't understand,' he muttered. 'You said those humans were going to kill me. But humans aren't like that, Squintum. I've never seen that man in the white coat before, but that girl – she was kind to me while I was in that place. And my own people at home – where I've always lived, before I got lost, that is – they've always been ever so good to me. Humans don't kill dogs, surely?'

'Sometimes they do,' said Squintum, and he explained everything about the Dogs' Home and places like it, and why, because people are either thoughtless or cruel, there are so many stray dogs abandoned by their owners.

'Too many to cope with,' he finished, 'so they just put them to sleep.'

'But I don't mind going to sleep,' said Lubber. 'In fact, I love it.'

'It's an expression,' said Squintum. 'They kill them. They were about to kill you. I saved you.'

'Oh,' said Lubber slowly. 'Oh, how can I ever thank you enough?'

'That remains to be seen,' said Squintum drily. 'In the meantime, are you hurt?'

'Hurt?'

'In case you didn't notice, you ran straight through a glass door.'

'Oh,' said Lubber.

He stood up and shook himself. Small pieces of glass flew out of his coat. 'No,' he said. 'I don't think so.'

'It's that thick hair of yours,' said Squintum.

And that thick head, he thought.

'They'll be angry, won't they?' said Lubber. 'The people at the Dogs' Home?'

'They will,' said Squintum, 'And not only with you. I think I'd better steer clear of the place for a while.'

'But don't you belong to someone?' asked Lubber. 'I do.'

Squintum chose not to answer the dog's question. Instead he said, 'Just now you mentioned your people at home. Whereabouts is your home?'

Lubber hung his head.

'I don't know,' he said.

The Siamese cat leaped nimbly up on to the balustrade that surrounded the covered bandstand. From this vantage point, he could see all around the park. He settled himself comfortably.

'Tell me, Lubber,' he said. 'How exactly did you come to be lost?'

Lubber sighed.

'I expect you think I'm a bit thick in the head,' he said.

'Oh, what an idea!' said Squintum. 'Why do you say such a thing?'

'Well, you must think it funny that I don't know where my home is. But you see, Squintum, it's nowhere near here. In fact, it must be hundreds of miles from this town.'

'You've walked hundreds of miles?'

'No. I rode.'

'In a car?'

'No. In a furniture van.'

'Start at the beginning,' said Squintum.

'Well,' said Lubber, 'I belong to two old ladies, sisters they are, and we live in a thatched cottage in a little village under a big hill. Ever so nice to me, they are – were – and I was as happy as could be. Mind you, their legs weren't too strong, even though they each had three of them.'

'Three legs each!' said Squintum.

Lubber's eyes twinkled under his bushy brows.

'Yes,' he said. 'Two ordinary ones and a wooden one. They both walked with a stick, you see. I was pulling *your* leg. Anyway, we never had to walk very far, which was a mercy.

I'm not too fond of exercise. What's more, I like to take a nap every now and then.'

He yawned.

'All that running's tired me out,' he said. 'Can't I tell you the rest later?'

'No,' said Squintum sharply. 'Go on.'

'One day,' said Lubber, 'the family in the house next door to our cottage were moving, you see, and this big furniture van came and parked outside. My old ladies had gone down to the shop at the other end of the village – I kept out of the way, it's a good quarter of a mile – and then it came on to rain and I couldn't get into the cottage. So I climbed into this furniture van. The removal men were inside the house – they'd finished loading everything and I expect they were having a cup of tea – so I thought I'd just shelter for a bit. Now one of the things in the van was a very comfy-looking sofa, and I suddenly felt like having forty winks. I dare say you can guess the rest.'

'They shut the doors and drove off,' said Squintum.

'That's right. Next thing I knew we were moving. I couldn't see out and I didn't know where we were going. I just hoped it wouldn't be too far, and then perhaps I could walk home.'

'That would have been very tiring, surely?' said Squintum.

'I suppose so,' said Lubber. 'But as it was, we went on and on for ages before at last they stopped and opened the doors and I jumped out and ran off. Like I said, I must be hundreds of miles from home. I wandered round the town for a bit, sleeping rough, you know, eating out of dustbins, that sort of thing, until a man in uniform caught me . . .'

'. . . the Dog Warden,' said Squintum.

'. . . and put me in that place where you live.'

'And where you nearly died.'

'Grrrrr!' said Lubber, shaking himself. 'Whatever am I to do, Squintum?'

The Siamese stood up on the balustrade of the bandstand and looked all around the park for possible danger. Seeing none, he stretched himself luxuriously, unsheathing his claws and dragging each forefoot in turn along the wooden rail with a rasping sound.

'Talk about needles in haystacks!' he said. 'A thatched cottage in a little village under a big hill. Gordon Bennett! There must be thousands of such cottages.'

'Ah, but wait!' said Lubber. 'I've just remembered. There's a White Horse on the hill. We can see it from our garden.'

'There must be thousands of white horses,' said Squintum. 'Anyway, the horse might have been moved to another place or sold or anything.'

'No, no! Not a live horse. A great picture of one, cut into the turf of the hillside.'

Squintum's tail-tip twitched.

'That's interesting,' he said. 'They don't

have such things in these northern parts. Must be chalk country. Looks as if we should head south.'

Lubber, who had lain down, exhausted by so much talking, sprang to his feet.

'"We"?' he said. 'D'you mean . . .?'

'Thought I might accompany you,' said Squintum. 'I can't say I'm very happy here, and I'm still young, and I've a good few lives left. Mind if I come along?'

'Mind?' barked Lubber. 'I should say not! Why, with you to help me, I might stand a better chance of finding my way home. And my old ladies would love you!'

What a nice sort of animal you are, he thought.

'But,' Lubber went on, 'I don't know why you should do this for me. I don't know why you saved my life this morning. Have you done that before, for other dogs?'

'No,' said Squintum.

'Why me?' said Lubber.

I don't really know, thought the Siamese. I just rather like you.

'Ask me no questions and I'll tell you no lies,' he said. 'And now get some sleep. I'll keep watch. As soon as darkness falls, we must be off.'

Chapter Three

'A GIRT EXPLOSION'

No one came near the bandstand that afternoon, and Lubber slept like a log. Squintum catnapped.

Darkness fell and the moon rose.

'On your feet!' said Squintum sharply.

'What. . .? why. . .? where. . .?' began Lubber as he obeyed.

'To answer your questions in order,' said Squintum. 'One, we're off. Two, because that's what you want. And three, to the thatched cottage in the little village under the big hill with the White Horse on it.'

He ran down the steps of the bandstand and set off for the park gates.

'But wait,' said Lubber, ranging alongside the padding Siamese. 'How do you know which way to go? How shall we know which way is south?'

Briefly Squintum raised his blue eyes to the glittering heavens, and stared at one especially brilliant point of light.

'We follow the Pole Star,' he said.

'I don't understand,' said Lubber.

'You wouldn't,' said Squintum. 'You're a dog, and dogs are daytime beasts. We cats are creatures of the darkness. We can read the night skies.'

Lubber too looked up.

'Is there only one Pole Star then?' he said.

'Two,' said Squintum. 'One for the South Pole, one for the North.'

Lubber considered this.

'But,' he said, 'we could be going in completely the wrong direction.'

Squintum gave one of his sudden harsh yowls. It could have been of surprise, or of amusement, or of annoyance at being asked so many questions, Lubber wasn't sure.

'Look,' said the Siamese. 'If the sun rises on our left tomorrow morning and sets on our right tomorrow evening, we're going the correct way. Just wait and see, eh? And now save your breath, there's a good dog. I want to be well clear of this town and deep in the countryside by dawn.'

And they were.

By first light, which was very early, for it was near to the longest day of the year, they had travelled perhaps a dozen miles from their starting-point. Squintum disdained such things as roads and struck straight across country, following his star, and then, when this had paled and vanished, trusting to some instinctive compass in his brain. Then the sun rose, on their left.

'You were right!' barked Lubber. 'We're going south! We're going home!' His bushy tail wagged wildly.

'Keep your hair on,' said Squintum. 'We've a long way to go yet. Let's have a rest.'

'Oh, let's!' cried Lubber.

They found an old deserted field-shed in the middle of nowhere, and Lubber flumped down anyhow on its floor of dusty straw. Squintum climbed into a manger half filled with frowsty hay, and curled himself comfortably.

A distant cow lowed, a late cuckoo called, and swallows flew in and out of the doorway, fetching insects to feed their young in their mud-nests under the roof. Dog and cat slept.

It was food, or rather the sound of food, that woke Squintum. The field-shed was full of mice, and the cat's keen ears caught the rustle of their movements. He slipped down from the manger.

In quite a short while, he caught and ate three, and lastly he found a nest of fat pink naked babies behind an old straw bale, and polished them off for afters. Then he fell to licking his paws and cleaning his face and combing his whiskers.

His grooming completed, he sat and looked at the untidy heap that was Lubber. I can feed myself, thought Squintum, but what about him? He's going to be ravenous when he wakes up.

Lubber stirred, got to his feet, stretched, and shook himself.

'I'm ravenous!' he said.

'I could catch you a mouse,' Squintum said.

'A mouse! I could eat a horse!'

At that moment they heard, not far off, the bang of a gun.

'We'd better be on our way,' said Squintum. 'I've no wish to be mistaken for a rabbit by some trigger-happy farmer.'

But before they could make a move there was a sudden whirr of wings, and in through the door of the field-shed flew a large bird; it landed clumsily on the top rail of the manger and perched there unsteadily, its beak wide open with shock and fear.

To Lubber it was just a bird, but the worldly-wise Squintum could see that it was a pigeon, and not an ordinary pigeon either. This was no wild bird nor a stray from a town square, but a racing pigeon, with long, slaty-blue, tapering wings, and on one pink leg a blue ring stamped with its number. This, though Squintum did not actually know it, was to identify the bird should it become lost

in its efforts to reach home. And this pigeon
certainly appeared to be lost. It looked about
it in a dazed way, and seemed unaware of any
possible danger from cat or dog.

'What is it?' said Lubber.

'It's a racing pigeon, a homer,' said Squintum. 'The owners take them a long, long way
away and then let them go, and each bird
knows instinctively exactly where its home
is. They race, you see, and the first one back
into its loft is the winner. This one isn't going
to win anything by the look of it.'

The look of the pigeon was just plain ap-
petizing to the hungry Lubber, but Squintum's
reaction, perhaps because he was full fed, was
one of simple curiosity.

'What's the matter, stranger?' he said. 'You
look scared out of your wits.'

For a moment the pigeon did not answer, but sat and panted, beak agape. Then it gasped, 'Man . . . gun . . . 'E nearly shot me!'

'Outside, quickly, Lubber!' hissed Squintum. 'See what you can see. If he catches us in here, we could all be dead ducks.'

'Ducks?' said Lubber. 'I don't see how . . .' he began, but the Siamese spat angrily at him, so he hurried outside. He was soon back.

'There is a man with a gun in the distance,' he said, 'but he's walking away from us.'

'I'm glad to hear that,' said the pigeon. 'That I am.'

It seemed to have recovered a little, and even began to preen its feathers. Out of them it picked a number of tiny round black objects.

'What are those?' said Lubber softly to Squintum.

'Shot,' said the cat. 'Pellets. He's had a narrow escape,' and to the bird he said, 'Are you wounded?'

The pigeon stretched one wing, slowly, to its full extent, and then the other.

'I don't reckon,' it said, 'but my head's buzzin' like a bees' nest. I thought I were a goner, I did. There I was, swingin' along nice and easy, only about a hundred mile to go to my loft, and next thing I know there's a girt explosion, right in my ear-'ole. That didn't half give me a shock, I'll tell you!'

'Squintum!' said Lubber in an excited voice, as the pigeon fell to hunting for more shot in its plumage.

'What?'

'You hear the way that bird talks? Its accent, I mean?'

'Yes. Very rural. A clodhopper, I should say.'

'Well, they talk like that in my part of the world! Where I come from! That bird might live quite close, maybe even in my village!'

'A hundred miles away,' said Squintum drily. 'And that's as the pigeon flies.'

'Yes, but if it knows exactly where its home is, like you said, maybe it could guide us.'

'Quite how we should keep up with a racing pigeon, I have no clear idea,' said Squintum. 'But there may be the germ of an interesting possibility there. It may be worth our while to befriend the creature rather than to eat it.'

'You must allow us to introduce ourselves,' he said to the pigeon in the politest of tones. 'I am called Squintum, and this is my friend Lubber.'

'How do?' said the pigeon.

'May we have the pleasure of knowing your name?'

The pigeon raised the leg with the blue ring on it, and scratched the side of its face.

'It's more of a number,' it said.

'Oh?'

'Ar. Eighty-two stroke seven o eight stroke KT, that's me.'

'82/708/KT?' said Squintum. 'Charming, charming! It does not however tell us to which sex you belong.'

'I be a hen,' said the pigeon.

'A hen?' said Lubber. 'I don't see how . . .?'

'A female pigeon,' said Squintum. 'And a very beautiful one, if I may say so.'

The pigeon gave a bubbling trill.

'I bet you do say that to all the girls,' she cooed.

'But,' said Squintum, 'your name is quite a . . . mouthful. Perhaps you would allow us to shorten it? May we just use the final letters, KT?'

'Don't make no odds to me,' said the pigeon.

'Katie it is then,' said Squintum. 'Now then, Katie, am I correct in thinking you to be a homing pigeon?'

'You're right.'

'And you are returning home, travelling south?'

'I was.'

'You were? You mean you've changed your mind?'

'I haven't changed it,' said Katie. 'That girt explosion changed it.'

'I don't follow,' said Lubber. 'Surely you can remember instinctively exactly where your home is?'

'I could,' said Katie. 'Trouble is, I been and gone and lost my memory.'

Chapter Four

THE BARBECUE

'That,' said Squintum, 'is too bad.'

He caught Lubber's eye.

'Please excuse us for a moment,' he said to the pigeon. 'We must just make sure that the coast is still clear.'

Outside, and out of the bird's hearing, Squintum spoke briefly and to the point. 'She's disoriented,' he said.

'Sorry?'

'Lost her sense of direction. No use to us. Might as well eat her.'

'Oh no!' said Lubber.

'Why not? Thought you were hungry.'

'I am, I am. But I couldn't kill her. The way she talks reminds me so much of home. And, anyway, the poor thing's only just escaped death.'

'Lubber,' said Squintum, 'when I first met you, I thought you were a bit soft in the head. I don't think that now – not so much anyway – but soft-hearted you certainly are. Come along now. We must get a move on.'

'But what about Katie?' said Lubber.

'What about Katie?'

'Well, shouldn't we at least say goodbye to her?'

Before the cat could answer, the pigeon came waddling out of the field-shed and walked trustingly up to them. Automatically, Squintum extended his claws, his tail-tip twitching, but Lubber stepped in front of him and said in a kindly voice, 'Well, Katie, it's been so nice meeting you and I hope you'll soon be better, but we must be off now. Goodbye.'

'Which way are you goin', Mr Lubber?' said Katie.

'South.'

'You gennulmen got any objections if I come along?'

'None at all!' said Lubber heartily.

Squintum sighed and sheathed his claws.

'Are you proposing to walk?' he said acidly.

Katie gave a bubbling trill of laughter.

'Oh, Mr Squintum!' she said. 'You and your little jokes! You'll be the death of me!'

Squintum passed his tongue over his lips.

'Walk indeed!' said Katie. 'I hope not! But I'd best make sure everything's workin',' and she took off and flew, a trifle unsteadily at first, and then more strongly. They watched as she gained height and began to fly around them in circles, each larger than the one before.

'What's she doing?' said Lubber.

'Trying to pick up her bearings,' said Squintum. 'If the shock wears off and her homing instinct returns, that'll be the last we shall see of her.'

But at that moment the pigeon broke off her circling and, with lifted wings, volplaned down to land beside them.

'Bit stiff at first, bruised, I expect,' said Katie, 'but I don't reckon I suffered much damage. Only to my head, it seems. Lost my sense of direction, I 'ave. Anyway, that shooter's gone, there's no sign of him.'

A look-out, thought Squintum. A scout. This bird could still be useful to us. To fly ahead and spy out the lie of the land and keep an eye out for possible danger.

'I am so glad, Katie,' he said in his silkiest tones, 'that you should wish to honour us with your company.'

Beneath all its hair, Lubber's face wore a look of astonishment.

As for Katie, she made a little bob.

'Oh, the honour's mine, Mr Squintum, sir,' she said.

'You see,' said Squintum, 'the three of us are, you might say, in the same boat.'

'In a boat?' said Lubber. 'I don't see how . . .?'

'That is to say,' continued Squintum, 'we are all heading south and we are all lost.'

'Lost?' said Katie. 'A clever gennulman like you?'

Squintum could not restrain a small purr of pleasure.

'Let me put it this way,' he said. 'Lubber –

Mr Lubber, that is – was taken from the bosom of his family by an unfortunate mischance.'

Katie looked puzzled.

'Sounds terrible,' she said.

'And I have volunteered to assist him in rediscovering his place of abode.'

'His place of a what?' said Katie.

'He's going to help me find my home,' said Lubber.

'But,' said Squintum, 'there are difficulties in our path. For example, we want to avoid contact with humans, who might wish to detain us out of the kindness of their hearts, or – for a great many humans are not kindhearted – to harm us. Secondly, we need to find sources of food, to sustain us. And, thirdly, it would be most useful to know what obstacles or hazards lie ahead – to know where a river might be crossed or a town avoided. In all these matters, my dear Katie, you could be of paramount assistance.'

'You reckon?' said Katie dazedly.

She looked at Lubber for help in interpreting this speech.

Lubber extracted from it what was, for him, the most important thing.

'Food,' he said. 'I need food. D'you think you could fly around and have a look? Red meat, that's what I want.'

Katie gave another of her little bobs.

'I'll find you something, Mr Lubber,' she said. 'Never you worry,' and off she flew. She circled once and then skimmed low over them.

'You gennulmen make a start, if you please,' she called down. 'I shall find you, sure enough.'

'Red meat!' sniffed Squintum as they set out. 'She'll likely bring you a worm.'

But, in fact, Fortune positively beamed upon them.

It was a beautiful summer's day, a Sunday, though none of them knew this, and everywhere people were relaxing in the sunshine. Just over the next hill beyond the field-shed, Katie found a village and looked down on house and cottage and bungalow. Everyone seemed to be out in their gardens, and in one, a very large garden belonging to a very large house, there was a swimming-pool. Some humans, large and small, were swimming in it, Katie could see, and some were lying beside it. Not far from the pool was a summer-house, in front of which stood a large, odd-looking contrivance on wheeled legs. Katie swooped down to investigate.

She had never in her life seen a barbecue and had no idea what it was, but there was no mistaking the array of meat, laid out ready for cooking when the bathers should feel like lunch.

There were thick steaks and fat chops and juicy kidneys for the grown-ups, and sausages and beefburgers for the children, enough to feed an army. Katie wheeled and was off at racing speed.

Twenty minutes later, Lubber and Squintum lay concealed behind a hedge. On the other side of it was the summer-house, on whose roof Katie was perched. Wonderful smells wafted to the sensitive noses of cat and dog.

Squintum had masterminded the plan of the robbery.

'You,' he said to Lubber, 'must eat everything you can, as quick as you can.'

'I will, I will!' said Lubber.

'Dogs are like that, I know – they bolt their food in the coarsest way and digest it later. Coming as I do from a more cultivated race, I cannot do that. I shall simply carry away the largest piece I can manage. And you, Lubber, when you have eaten all you can hold, must do the same. Take away with you the biggest bit you can grip in your jaws. As for you,

38

Katie, you must keep up the diversion for as long as you can, if possible until you hear the signal.'

'I'll fool 'em, never you fear, Mr Squintum,' said Katie. 'You just give the word.'

This Squintum now did.

He yowled softly, too softly to be heard by the laughing, splashing humans, and at the sound Katie took off from the summer-house roof and flew up over the swimming-pool.

Though she was an almost pure-bred racer, one of her ancestors had been a tumbler, a variety of aerobatic pigeon, and she now put on a dramatic show. From high above the pool she suddenly dropped, twisting and turning and somersaulting and spinning like a falling leaf.

'Oh look!' cried the bathers. 'Look at that bird!'

'It can't fly properly!'

'It's been hurt!'

'It's been shot!'

'Look out, it's going to land in the water!'

But with a few feet to spare, Katie righted herself to make what looked like a forced landing on the pool side. Here she stumbled about, dragging one wing, the very picture of a sorely injured pigeon.

The English are reputed to be a nation of animal lovers, but, as Squintum had foreseen, the bathers reacted in very different ways.

'Poor thing!'

'Oh, it's only an old pigeon.'

'We must help it!'

'Knock it on the head, I should.'

'Put it out of its misery.'

'Don't be so horrible!'

'Be nice under a pie-crust with a bit of bacon.'

'Can I have it for a pet, Mummy?'

'Can I have a shot at it with your air-rifle, Daddy?'

'We must take it to the vet. Catch it, someone.'

But somehow every time someone was just about to catch the pigeon, it managed to struggle a little further off. Until suddenly, from the direction of the summer-house, there came a loud bark, and at this signal the pigeon jumped lightly into the air and flew easily away.

Like Old Mother Hubbard's cupboard, the barbecue was bare.

Chapter Five

HORSEVIEW COTTAGE

In a thatched cottage in a little village under a big hill with a White Horse on it, Miss Bun and Miss Bee sat drinking cocoa. Miss Bun was eating one of her favourite biscuits, Custard Creams, and Miss Bee one of hers, Garibaldis.

Long ago, eighty and seventy-eight years respectively, to be precise, the two sisters had been christened Margaret and Beatrice, but their parents had usually called them Bunty and Beatie. Gradually these names became shortened to Bun and Bee, and everybody in the village (where everything is known about

everyone else) always referred to them as
'Miss Bun and Miss Bee'.

'Oh, Bee,' said Miss Bun sadly, 'how I wish
we knew where he was.'

'Oh, Bun,' replied Miss Bee, 'how I hope
that he is still somewhere.'

Both sisters looked up at a framed photo-
graph that hung on the kitchen wall. It was
an enlarged snapshot of Lubber as a puppy,
lying on the lawn, asleep of course.

'Even if he is alive,' said Miss Bun, 'we
shall never see him again, shall we?'

'Not after all this time,' said Miss Bee. 'He's
been gone weeks.'

Miss Bun drained her cocoa.

'Ah well,' she said. 'Time for our game.'

Like many elderly folk, Miss Bun and Miss
Bee were great creatures of habit, and their
days followed an exact pattern. Each of these
days, of course, ended with bedtime, and lately
this had presented the sisters with a problem. What with rheumatism and arthritis and
suchlike things, neither was too steady on her
pins. And the stairs at Horseview Cottage
were very steep.

On the flat Miss Bun and Miss Bee, short,
sturdy, tubby people both, did pretty well.
They walked arm in arm as they had done
since childhood, but now each had a walking-
stick in her outer hand. Miss Bun (whose left
leg was the stronger) walked on the right,
Miss Bee (whose right leg was the stronger)
on the left. It was thus that the villagers

always saw them, like a pair of six-legged Siamese twins.

Now a gentle walk to the village or a stroll in the garden was one thing, but climbing the staircase was quite a different matter, and getting to bed at night became a very difficult business, where neither sister could help the other.

Miss Bun and Miss Bee consulted their friends, one of whom told them that there was a device on the market called a chair-lift. This could be installed at the side of the staircase, and would carry them, one at a time, up or down.

'All you have to do,' said the friend, 'is to sit on a comfy little seat and press a switch, and this thing will carry one of you up to the top of the stairs without you moving a muscle.

43

Then out you get and press another switch to send the seat down again for the other one.'

So Miss Bun and Miss Bee had this wonderful machine fitted and it worked a treat, and what fun it was, such fun that at first they spent hours riding up and down on it, sending their electricity bill sky-high. But it still left them with a problem at the day's end. Who should go to bed first? This, after all, would be a great advantage, giving one or other of them first go at the bathroom and the certainty of being the first to be snuggled down in bed, while the unlucky one was left with the chores of locking up and putting out lights.

All through their long lives together, Miss Bun had never taken advantage of the fact that she was the elder, nor would Miss Bee have allowed her to do so, and simply taking turns to ride upstairs first would, they thought, be boring. So they decided to play for it.

Each evening, after their cocoa and biscuits, Miss Bun and Miss Bee would sit opposite one another at the kitchen table and solemnly play a game, one of the games that they had played together seventy years before.

Sometimes it was Snap, sometimes Beggar My Neighbour or Happy Families, but always it was conducted with the greatest seriousness, until at last one or other would give a little cry of triumph. Then she would hobble to the foot of the stairs, sit on the seat, press the switch and, smiling broadly both at the victory and the sensation, glide happily aloft. On this particular night, Miss Bun was the lucky one.

'Mrs Dose the Doctor's wife, if you please, Bee,' she said, 'and' (with special relish) 'Miss Bun the Baker's daughter, and I'm the winner!'

It was a warm night, a night of the full moon, and Miss Bun did not get into bed when she was ready, but stood by the window in her flannelette nightgown (pink with white roses), her silver hair in a long braid, looking out to the big hill that rose above the little village. She waited till her sister, in her flannelette nightgown (blue with yellow daisies), her hair in two neat pigtails, came to stand beside her, and they leaned comfortably on one another, to ease the weight on their bad legs.

Together they stared at the shape of the great White Horse opposite them.

'It's funny,' said Miss Bun, 'but I sometimes think he's up there.'

'On the Horse?' said Miss Bee.

'Yes. You could see him tonight if he was there, the moon's so bright.'

'I sometimes think that too. But it's hard to imagine him walking that far.'

'And uphill too.'

'Lazy old thing.'

'But so sweet-natured, wasn't he?'

'Wasn't he! Shall we ever have another dog, d'you think, Bun?'

'I shouldn't like to, Bee.'

'Just in case he should come back one day, you mean?'

'Yes, and find someone else in his place.'

For a moment longer, the sisters stared at the huge moonlit form of the White Horse.

'Magical, isn't it?' said Miss Bee.

'And magic makes miracles,' said Miss Bun.

'And miracles do happen,' they said with one voice.

Then they turned and smiled at each other, rather ruefully, and sighed, and climbed into their beds.

Chapter 6

TO FIND A
MOTORWAY

Flying at about a hundred feet, for her recent experience of gunfire had made her wary of low altitudes, Katie could see the thieves running away, southward of course. The cat bounded neatly over the short sun-dried summer grass, his head held high against the weight of something carried in his mouth. The big dog galloped awkwardly, tripping now and again over what looked to the pigeon like some sort of rope, one end of which he had in his jaws.

They crossed a couple of large fields and disappeared from sight into a small copse. Katie circled, watching, but they did not emerge on the other side, so, after one more circuit to make sure there was no danger, she dropped quickly down in among the trees.

She pitched upon a low branch, beneath which Lubber and Squintum lay side by side. Squintum had taken as his spoils a large juicy piece of fillet steak, and this he now ate, delicately, without hurry, biting off a bit at a time and licking it luxuriously with his rasping tongue, before getting to work with his needle-sharp white teeth. He was relishing every mouthful.

Lubber, Katie could see despite his hairiness, looked a good deal fatter and small wonder. In the short time that Katie's diversionary tactics had taken, he had polished off the meat set out to feed a party of a dozen adults and as many children. Now he lay sprawled, groaning a little at the pressure of the food inside him. Beside him lay what had looked from high above like a rope. It was, Katie could now see, a long pink string of sausages.

For a while no one spoke. Then Squintum, swallowing a final mouthful, said simply, 'Excellent!'

Lubber belched loudly. 'Have a sausage,' he said.

'Decent of you,' said Squintum, 'but I'm F.T.B.'

'F.T.B.?'

'Full to the brim.'

'Me, too,' said Lubber happily, and he stretched out and went to sleep.

Squintum sat, licking his paws and cleaning his face, and when he had finished, he turned his blue eyes up to the pigeon sitting above him.

'My dear Katie,' he said, 'how can we ever thank you?'

Katie bobbed on the branch.

'Oh, don't mention it, Mr Squintum, sir,' she said.

'But,' said Squintum, 'here we are, replete, and you have not eaten. I don't imagine you could fancy a sausage?'

'Oh no, thank you kindly,' said Katie, 'but I could do with summat to eat, no doubt about it.'

'Such as?' said Squintum.

'Corn,' said the pigeon. 'A good cropful of wheat, now that's the stuff to put feathers on your chest.'

'Is there any near?'

'Oh ah, Mr Squintum, there's wheatfields all about this time of year, comin' ripe for harvest. I shan't go short nohow. What d'you know, talkin' about it's made me even more hungry! Will you two gennulmen excuse me if I pop out for a quick snack and a drink?'

'Watch out for farmers with guns,' said Squintum.

'I will, never you mind! And I'll have a good look round, make sure no one's comin' after us, see what lies ahead,' said Katie. 'So long!' and up she flew.

Squintum lay beside the sleeping dog and thought.

So far, so good, he said to himself. We've put a few miles behind us, we've picked up a useful ally, and we're well fed; better, I suspect, than we shall be again for many a day. But there is without doubt a very long way to go, even supposing we are lucky enough in the end to find the thatched cottage in the little village under the big hill with the White Horse on it. And let's face it, I am the only one who is going to give the matter any thought. Unless the bird recovers her homing instinct, she is useless in that respect, and Lubber here is much too happy-go-lucky a chap to worry his hairy head about the outcome. He simply trusts me to perform a miracle and take him home. If only we could travel south as fast as he travelled north in that furniture van.

Squintum sat up sharply.

That's it, he thought. We'll get a lift! But how? Stand by the southbound side of a main road and put my paw in the air? No telling where we'd finish up, probably back in a home for strays. No, there's no way we could hitch-hike, but maybe we could be stowaways, just as Lubber was. It'd have to be in something like a heavy lorry, where we could get aboard without the driver's knowledge. But all the heavy lorries use the motorways, where they're not allowed to stop.

'But wait!' said Squintum out loud. 'They do!'

The squally voice woke Lubber, who opened an eye and said, 'Who do?'

'Go back to sleep,' said Squintum, and when Lubber had promptly obeyed, he continued his train of thought. The big lorries *do* stop, at the motorway service stations. I remember seeing that when I was sold as a kitten and my breeder was driving me down to the Dogs' Home. The drivers stop there to fill their lorries with fuel, and themselves with tea and butties in the service station restaurant. That would be the time! Worth a try, surely? All we need is to find a motorway, and that's something Katie ought to be able to do. She should be back soon.

Even as Squintum thought this, there was a noise of flapping wings and then a crackle of twigs, as not one, but two pigeons, landed in the tree above.

'Hello, Katie,' called the Siamese. 'Found a friend, have you?'

There was a moment's silence, and then a voice said, 'By gum, did you hear that, lad?'

'Ay, I did,' said another voice. 'But don't fret thyself. It's only an old cat.'

Squintum was no expert on regional accents, but he could clearly hear a difference between these broad Yorkshire voices and Katie's Wiltshire dialect. He squinted up and saw that the speakers were a pair of fat wood-pigeons.

Katie he had spared, for a reason, but these birds deserved no such mercy, and he leaped across the slumbering Lubber and shot up the tree-trunk towards them.

'Watch tha step!' shouted one. 'T'old moggy's after us. Stir thy stumps, lad!' and with a great clatter of wings, they burst up through the canopy and flew away.

The noise woke Lubber. He looked around

and could see no sign of the cat.

'Squintum!' he barked loudly. 'Where are you?'

'Up here!' spat Squintum, angry at missing. 'And keep your voice down, do!'

He ran down the trunk and began to stalk away, lashing his tail.

'Where are you going?' asked Lubber.

'To look for that Katie.'

Lubber hesitated. On the one hand, he did not want to be left behind, so dependent was he on the cat. On the other hand, he did not want to leave the string of sausages which, now that he had had time to digest the rest of the meat, was looking most attractive.

'Shall I come?' he said.

'No,' said Squintum.

'You won't be long?'

'No,' said Squintum.

'Shall I keep you a sausage?'

'No,' said Squintum.

So Lubber took the end sausage of the string in his mouth and began to chew. And, curiously enough, the next sausage seemed anxious to follow its neighbour, and the next, and the next, until, quite soon, there was only one sausage left.

I suppose I really ought to keep it for him, thought Lubber, in case he changes his mind, but while he was thinking this, somehow the last sausage disappeared too.

Squintum sat at the edge of the copse, watching the skies. They were cloudless and, high above him, a number of inland gulls were rising effortlessly on a thermal, their white wings spread. Swallows and martins flew busily in pursuit of insects, and a long way above them, higher even than the circling gulls, coal-black swifts cut through the clear summer air on their sickle-shaped wings.

How pleasant to be a bird, thought Squintum. If Lubber and I could only fly, how quickly we could complete our journey.

Then he saw Katie coming, racing towards him at a fine rate. Catching sight of the waiting cat, she dropped down and landed beside him. Squintum could see that her crop was bulging.

'Aah! That's better, Mr Squintum, sir!' she said. 'That ought to keep me goin' for a while. I feel quite my old self again.'

'D'you mean to say that you've got your sense of direction back?' said Squintum.

'Wish I had,' said Katie, 'but that shooter never done me no good. It's comin' back a bit – I think I know which direction home is. But I couldn't fly straight to it, not to save my life.'

Despite himself, Squintum passed his tongue across his lips at these last words, so strong a thing is instinct. He controlled his thoughts.

'Tell me, Katie,' he said, 'do you know what I mean by a motorway?'

'That I do, Mr Squintum,' said Katie. 'Hugeous girt roads, full of cars and coaches and lorries. Hear the noise of the traffic from ever so high up, I can. They run right across the country, for hundreds and hundreds of miles. We pigeons use 'em for aids to navigation. Supposin' I get blown a bit off course by a strong wind, or just lose my bearings for a minute, I say to myself, "Where've you got to, 82/708/KT?" and then I look down and see a girt motorway, and that tells me I'm too far this way or that. Matter of fact, there's a motorway not too far from where I do live. Runs due east and west, it does.'

'But some run north and south, don't they?' said Squintum. 'It's south we want to go.'

'Oh ar,' said Katie. 'There's two girt long 'uns that run north and south, one each side of the country.'

'Anywhere near here?'

'I dunno, I'm sure.'

'But you could find out, you could find a motorway for us, could you, Katie?'

'I reckon. Might take a bit of flyin', unless there's one handy. Which there might be, you never know. Why, Mr Squintum? What d'you want a motorway for? Surely you're not going to walk down one of them?'

'No, no,' said Squintum, and he explained to the pigeon the idea that he had in mind.

'Think how fast we could get south!' he finished.

'Oh ar,' said Katie. 'They do travel, even the big lorries do. I reckon to do sixty mile an hour with a following wind, but I can't keep up with they.'

'You wouldn't need to,' said Squintum. 'You

could ride too.'

'It's an idea and no mistake,' said Katie.

'Worth a try, surely?' said Squintum.

'Give us a bit of time to digest this cropful of wheat,' said Katie, 'and I'll go and have a look. Visibility's good today; I should be able to see a long way.'

'A bird's-eye view,' said Squintum thoughtfully.

'Ar,' said Katie. 'It's surprisin' what you can see from a height.'

'Have you ever seen a white horse?'

The pigeon gave a bubbling trill of amusement.

'A white horse?' she said. 'Why, bless you, I've seen white 'uns, black 'uns, brown 'uns, spotted 'uns, all sorts!'

'No, I don't mean a live horse. I mean a picture of one, a huge picture, cut into the turf so that the chalk shows up white.'

'Oh there's several of those about. There's one not so far from where I do live.'

'On a big hill?' said the Siamese.

'Ar.'

'Is there a little village under the hill?'

'Ar.'

'Is there a thatched cottage in the village?'

'More'n likely. I dunno for sure. I've never looked.'

'But you could do it, couldn't you, Katie?' said Squintum. 'Once we get near enough?'

'Do what, Mr Squintum?'

'Find the White Horse.'

Chapter Seven

DESERTED

'Once we gets into chalk country, I'll find you a white horse all right, Mr Squintum,' said Katie confidently. 'Might take time.'

'We have plenty of that. You use some of it now – to digest your food. And talking of food, I fancy a sausage,' said Squintum, and he turned and disappeared into the copse.

His first impulse, on finding that Lubber had scoffed the lot, was to wake the greedy beast and bawl him out. But that won't bring the sausages back, said Squintum to himself. And we can't move on until Katie reports about motorways. So I might as well take it easy. And he curled himself against the big dog's hairy stomach and closed his blue eyes.

An hour passed, while Squintum dozed and Lubber snored, and then came the sound of wings and a crackle of twigs overhead. Squintum was instantly alert to the chance of bagging another Yorkshire woodpigeon, but it was Katie.

'We're in luck,' she said.

'You've found one?' said Squintum.

Lubber opened an eye.

'Found what?' he said.

'A motorway,' said Katie.

'A motorway?' said Lubber. 'I don't see how . . .?'

'I'll explain in a minute,' said Squintum. 'How far, Katie?'

'No more than five or six mile away as the pigeon flies. Due west, cross country. What do you think of that then?'

'Brilliant!'

'And that's not all.'

'Don't tell me you've found us a horse as well?'

'A horse?' said Lubber. 'I don't see how . . .?'

'No, no,' said Katie. 'I found what you was talkin' about, Mr Squintum. You musta had your sixth sense workin' overtime!'

'A service station!' cried Squintum.

'I reckon. Buildings and petrol pumps and that by the side of the motorway, and folk pullin' off in their cars and gettin' out of 'em, and as for girt heavy lorries, why, there were dozens of them.'

'82/708/KT,' said Squintum. 'You're a duck!'

'A duck?' said Lubber. 'I don't see how . . .?'

'Save your breath,' said Squintum. 'We're off!'

As cross-country travellers, the trio were not well matched. Squintum, for example, could creep through small holes in thick hedges or through the mesh of sheep-wire, where Lubber could not.

Lubber could leap obstacles or push his way through standing corn or thick undergrowth where Squintum was at a disadvantage.

Katie, airborne and free of all obstacles, could travel at ten times the speed of the other two.

But they soon settled into a routine.

The pigeon would fly ahead, watched by cat and dog, and then perch, on a tall tree or other vantage point, until they caught up with her. Sometimes these hops of hers were barely a hundred yards in length, but where the going was easy and the countryside open, she would often fly on a quarter of a mile or more.

Before long, they came upon a country lane at a point where it joined a main road. Katie had flown forward a little way, and Lubber and Squintum lay concealed in some long grass, waiting to cross when the traffic should allow. Above their heads, a signpost spread its four arms.

Had either animal been able to read, they would have found that the northern-pointing arm (the direction from which they had come) said WOODSETTS, the southern arm THORPE SALVIN & HARTHILL, the eastern WORKSOP and the western SHEFFIELD & M1 MOTORWAY.

For a moment there was a pause in the

stream of passing vehicles.

'Come on!' said Squintum, and they dashed across the A57 and into open fields once more.

Now, as Katie led them due west, the going became easier, and after a couple more miles they could actually hear the distant roar of the motorway traffic. A mile more, and they could see the motorway itself, and, almost directly ahead of them, the buildings of the service station.

As they drew nearer, they could see the pigeon sitting on the roof of the restaurant. They could also see that the entire compound was surrounded by a high wire fence, its mesh far too small to admit the slenderest of Siamese cats, let alone a large hairy mongrel dog.

'It's all fenced round,' said Lubber.

Squintum spat angrily. I should have known, he thought, that anything to do with motorways would have to be guarded against straying animals. At that moment, Katie flew down to join them.

'What are you goin' to do now, Mr Squintum?' she asked. ''Tis all fenced round.'

Squintum spat again, his tail lashing. What were they to do?

But then Lubber, whose sight was keener than the cross-eyed cat's, said, 'I can see a gate in the wire.'

They moved cautiously forward to the edge of a concrete approach-road, and there, sure enough, was a large double gate, bearing a notice that read:

> ## M1 WOODALL SERVICES
> ## EMERGENCY ENTRANCE
> ## FOR POLICE USE ONLY

It was firmly shut.

'It's shut,' said Lubber.

'You have a talent,' said Squintum acidly, 'for stating the obvious.'

For once, good-natured Lubber reacted angrily to the cat's patronizing tone. 'You have a talent,' he growled, 'for making catty remarks. And I'm not as stupid as I look. Sooner or later someone will open it. That's the thing about gates, you see – humans put them there to get in and out by. All we have to do is wait,' and he lay down, put his head on his paws, and went to sleep.

'What do you know?' said Katie. 'Mr Lubber's right,' and she settled herself comfortably in a nearby bush.

Squintum sat and waited, with the infinite patience of his kind. Lubber is right, he told himself, once his frustration had died down. We must just wait, no matter how long it takes.

In fact, it took a long time.

Not till dusk had fallen and the motorway was ablaze with headlights did anything come near their hiding-place. Then suddenly a car drove past them and stopped, its lights shining full on the gate.

'Quick! Wake up!' hissed Squintum to the

sleepers, and he watched intently as a man in a blue uniform, wearing a peaked cap, got out and unlocked and opened the gate.

'Now!' said Squintum softly, and as the policeman got back into the driving-seat, all three animals slipped in past the near side of the patrol car. They hid in the shadows until it had driven past and away, and then looked round to get their bearings. They were, it seemed, on the edge of the service station's public car-park. This was brightly lit, but it was now too dark for Katie to find where the lorry-park might be.

'Pop up on that roof where you were before,' Squintum told her, 'and join us again at first light.'

'I can smell food,' said Lubber when the pigeon had gone, 'over there,' and he pointed with lifted muzzle.

'That'll be the restaurant,' said Squintum. 'You going to walk in there and sit up and beg?'

'No,' said Lubber, 'but there'll be dustbins outside. Humans are ever so wasteful of food.'

'Dustbins have lids.'

'Lids come off easy – no problem.'

'Worth a try, surely?' said Squintum.

Side by side, they began to slink along the inside of the perimeter fence, when suddenly a car drove in from the motorway. Instead of stopping near the restaurant, as most had done, it went quickly to the furthest part of the car-park and stopped there. In it, Lubber and Squintum could see, were a man and a

63

woman, and as the animals watched, the man got out. He looked about him, furtively it seemed, saw no one, took from his pocket a length of stout twine and opened a rear door. A dog leaped down and jumped up against the man's legs, licking at his hand and wagging its tail joyfully. Hastily the man fastened the twine to its collar, led it to the fence, and there tied the other end of the cord to an iron stanchion. Then he turned and hastened, ran, indeed, back to the car.

The dog had followed him trustingly to the fence, and even now, for a few seconds, it stood and wagged, watching its owner. But then it began to whine anxiously as the car's engine was restarted, and then to bark, frantically, as the man drove fast, out of the car-park and away to rejoin the motorway. And as the car disappeared from sight, there came, above the ceaseless roar of the passing traffic, a dreadful, doleful, heartbroken howling.

'Wait for me!' cried the tethered dog, straining and pulling madly at the end of the length of twine. 'Don't leave me! Come back! Oh, wait for me!'

Left to himself, Squintum would probably have passed by on the other side, but the terrible wailing was more than the soft-hearted Lubber could bear and he galloped to the rescue.

At his approach, the howling changed to a frightened yap.

Lubber slid to a halt and stood waving his

bushy tail and giving a smily look from under his hairy eyebrows.

'Everything's going to be all right,' he said comfortingly. 'Don't be scared, old chap.'

'I'm not a chap,' said the other in a voice that trembled. 'And everything's not going to be all right. Everything's terribly wrong. My owners – they just left me here. Why? Why have they deserted me?'

Lubber looked down at the dog, who, he could now see, appeared very young, not much more, in fact, than a puppy.

'Oh, they'll come back for you,' he said. 'They just forgot, I expect. When they realize, they'll turn back.'

'Forget it,' said a voice, and Squintum appeared. 'The motorway's like life,' he said. 'There's no turning back.'

Chapter Eight

DOWN THE M1

The moon was now fully up and by its light Lubber and Squintum could clearly see the abandoned dog. Youthful she might be, and gangling in build, but she was tall, almost as tall as Lubber. Like Lubber, her ears were droopy and her tail long and plumy, but here the resemblance ended. It was not simply a difference of her coat – silky and wavy, and her colour – a rich red. It was an air about her, of elegance, of distinction, of breeding.

To the blue-blooded Squintum, this was instantly obvious.

To Lubber, she was simply a dog in distress, and his first thought was to release her from the tether against which she still strained, whining and staring at the spot where the car had disappeared.

'We'll soon have you free!' he growled, and was about to chop through the twine when Squintum hissed at him, 'No, Lubber, no!'

'Why not?'

'Let her free now and she's a dead dog.

She'll run straight on to the motorway, trying to follow her owners. Wait a little, and let's see if we can calm her down a bit. Ask her some questions, to distract her. Ask her what breed she is. Politely, mind.'

Lubber cleared his throat.

'I say!' he said in a jolly voice. 'I hope you won't mind if I ask – I mean, I ought to know but I've never actually seen anyone quite like you before – most attractive, that silky coat, and such a lovely colour – what I mean to say is, what kind of dog are you?'

'I'm a Red Setter.'

'Oh,' said Lubber. 'Er . . . pedigree, eh?'

'Of course.'

Squintum purred.

'What kind of dog are you?' said the Red Setter bitch.

'Well, I'm not really sure,' said Lubber. 'My mother was a cow-dog, there are lots of cows where I come from.'

'And your father?'

'Well, I'm not really sure.'

'What's your name?'

'Lubber. Oh, and this is my friend Squintum. What's yours?'

'I haven't got one.'

'But surely . . . those people who left you here, they must have called you something?'

'They never decided. They couldn't agree. They hadn't had me very long, you see.'

'How long?'

'A week.'

'But why . . .?' began Lubber, when Squintum interrupted.

'Look,' he said, 'there's plenty of time, we've the whole night before us. Why don't we ask our friend here just to lie down quietly and tell us all about herself, and then we'll see what we can do to help her? Worth a try, surely?'

'OK,' said Lubber. 'If you feel like it, that is . . . er . . . oh, it's awkward, you not having a name.'

The young Setter bitch, who had by now stopped pulling and whining, lay down as Squintum had suggested and looked at the large hairy mongrel dog, sighed deeply, and said, 'Why don't you give me one?'

'Oh gosh!' said Lubber. 'I'm no good at that sort of thing. Squintum here's the brainy one. He'd be better at it.'

'Well now,' said Squintum smoothly, 'let's think. Something to do with your breed, perhaps? A Red Setter, you said?'

'Yes. Irish Setters, some people call us.'

'Really! An Irish colleen!'

'That's nice!' said Lubber. ' "Colleen"! I like it, do you?'

A little wag of the long red tail signified assent, so Squintum said quickly, 'Go on then, Colleen. Tell us about yourself.'

The story was easily told. The bitch had at first been kept on by her breeder who had intended to show her, but he'd later changed his mind and sold her as a pet.

'To those people who dumped you here?'

asked Lubber.

'Yes,' said Colleen.

'After only a week? Why? Why didn't they like you? My old ladies loved me. What did you do wrong?'

'I don't really know,' said Colleen. 'I did howl at night a bit, because I was homesick. And I did nip their little boy once – he kept pulling my tail and it hurt.'

'Is that all?'

'Well . . . I did have a couple of accidents.'

'Accidents?'

'On the carpet. But really, I did want to please them. They were my owners. I didn't mean to be bad.'

'Bad?' growled Lubber. 'It's not you who are bad. To desert you and just drive off! I wouldn't have believed there were humans as wicked as that!'

'I would,' said Squintum.

'Listen, Colleen,' he said. 'Listen to a cat who is certainly older and possibly wiser than you. There are people who are fit to keep dogs and there are people who are not. You – whatever happens to you in the future – have had a lucky escape. Just now you are unhappy because you think that you have been a disappointment to your owners, and that it is your duty to go back to them and try to do better. If Lubber here were to chew through that twine, you might still want to follow them. First of all, you wouldn't have a cat in hell's chance of ever finding them. Second, you'd be a fool to try. And third, if you do try, you'll be run over and killed before you've gone half a mile. Have you understood what I'm saying to you?'

'Yes,' said Colleen, quietly now. 'But what am I to do? I'm homeless.'

'So are we!' said Lubber. 'But we're going to find a home – mine! Come with us! My old ladies would love you!' and he grabbed the twine in his teeth and bit through it. 'Come on!' he said. 'We're going to the dustbins to find some grub,' and he walked off, Squintum following.

For a moment, the Red Setter hesitated uncertainly. Then she ran after them.

Lubber's dustbin technique was simple but effective. First, he nosed off the lid. Then he stood against the rim and tipped the bin over. Humans, it seemed, were even more wasteful in motorway restaurants and cafeterias than in their own homes, and the pickings were good.

Lubber would happily have stayed snuffling about among the rubbish all night, but Squintum was fearful of discovery.

'Come away now,' he said to the two dogs, 'before someone finds us. We'll lie up till morning.'

They found a secluded corner at the back of a storage building, on to the roof of which Squintum climbed.

*

Flying out at first light, Katie soon spotted the cat and landed beside him. 'Morning, Mr Squintum, sir,' she said. 'Where be Mr Lubber?'

Squintum stretched and yawned.

'Below,' he said.

Katie peered over the edge of the roof.

'Well I never!' she said. 'Who's that with him then?'

'She's called Colleen,' said Squintum. 'She's coming with us.'

Katie gave her bubbling trill of amusement.

'He's a fast worker, Mr Lubber is!' she said. 'Fancy pickin' up a nice-lookin' girlfriend in a motorway service station! How'd she get here?'

'It's a long story,' said Squintum, looking up at the lightening sky, 'and there's no time for it now. Go and find the lorry-park, quick as you can.'

Ten minutes later, the four of them were assembled under the body of a giant lorry, one of a number whose drivers had stopped for an early breakfast.

'You three stop here,' said Squintum, 'while I have a look round,' and off he slunk.

At first it looked as though his plan would come to nothing. Each lorry that he investigated had its rear doors firmly closed, and even had they been open, the tailboards were too high. He might have scrambled up, the bird could have flown in, but the dogs could never have made such a leap. In fact, it was almost midday before Squintum found what he wanted.

A big articulated lorry pulled in, the load on its trailer covered with a huge tarpaulin sheet under which they could crawl; and, as luck would have it, it parked next to a loading-platform that was level with the lorry bed; all they had to do was to climb the steps of the platform and walk aboard. He went to fetch the others.

Had they been able to read, they would have learned two interesting things about this particular articulated lorry. First, they would have seen, in large letters on the door of the tug:

> J. DAVIDSON
> NIGHTLY TRUNK
> LEEDS–LONDON

Second, once they were safely under the tarpaulin, among dozens of cardboard boxes arranged on pallets, they would have known that each box contained

50 TINS 'BONZO' TOP-QUALITY DOG MEAT.

As it was, they lay in innocence both of the contents of the boxes and of their destination, and then they heard the engine start up and felt the artic move out, and then pick up speed on the motorway.

'This is the life!' said Squintum. 'Every hour that passes, we'll be sixty miles further south.'

'Without liftin' a wing!' said Katie.

Colleen lay shivering, appalled by the noise and the swaying motion. 'I'm scared,' she said.

Lubber licked her nose. 'I'll look after you,' he said. 'Just try and relax.'

'Look at that,' said Katie softly. 'Don't they make a lovely pair!'

Two hours passed.

Squintum was watchful, Colleen dozed uneasily, Katie fell into a light sleep and Lubber into a heavy one.

Then the engine note changed, the motion lessened, and the trailer swayed as the artic driver pulled off the motorway, parked and switched off. They heard the door of the tug slam, and then the sound of footsteps walking away.

'He's stopped for a cuppa,' said Squintum. 'Wake up, everyone. Katie, can you try to find out where we are?'

Katie slipped out from beneath the tarpaulin to find herself in the lorry-park of just such a service station as the one they had left a couple of hours earlier. The only difference, had she been able to read the sign, was its name.

M1 TODDINGTON SERVICES

Katie flew up above the motorway and immediately she felt that there was something wrong. Maybe it was the position of the sun or the direction of the prevailing wind, or maybe, she thought, my homin' instinct's comin' back a bit, but we're goin' wrong, I feel sure. We're too far east or my name's not 82/708/KT.

The higher she flew, the surer she felt that they must get out of here, that if they stayed in the artic they would be carried further and further away from their hoped-for destination.

At that moment, she saw a flight of homing pigeons racing along, following the exact line of the M1 and she put on speed to intercept them.

As they swept up to her, she flew alongside

them.

'Which way be us going, ladies and gennulmen, can you tell me?' she cried.

'Cor lumme luvaduck!' they called to one another.

'Proper old mangel-wurzel, ain't she, mate?'

'Talk about a country bumpkin!'

'We're goin' to the Smoke, me old china, that's where we're goin'.'

'The Smoke?' said Katie. 'Whatever do you mean?'

'London Town!' cried the racers. 'Down the old M1 to London Town!'

'To Lunnon!' cried Katie in horror. 'Oh, my heavens, we don't want to go there!' and she wheeled and went racing back.

Chapter Nine

LONG ODDS

Racing was what Miss Bun and Miss Bee were watching, at that moment, on the TV in Horseview Cottage.

For a long time, they had resisted having the television. They suspected (rightly) that much of it was taken up with panel games (which they would not understand), with situation comedies (which they would not find funny), and with the News (which they were sure would be all about war and famine and disasters).

'The only thing we should enjoy,' they said to one another, 'would be the weather forecast.'

'And, anyway,' they said, 'one of those ugly aerials would quite spoil the look of our roof.'

But then quite recently a friend, the one who had suggested the chair-lift, persuaded them that it really would be worth their while to have a set, if only to see the wonderful natural history programmes, since both were so fond of animals.

'And make sure you get a remote control,' the friend said, 'so that you can change channels or switch on and off without having to get up out of your chairs.'

The friend was right – Miss Bun and Miss Bee loved the animal programmes. And the sisters were right – they didn't at all like the panel games or the situation comedies or the grim news, but they did very much enjoy using the remote control to switch them off. 'Zapping', they called it, and whichever sister had the thing in her hand would point it at the set, and narrow her eyes like a gunfighter, and press the off switch with a cry of 'ZAP!' Then they would look at one another and giggle like young girls.

But the biggest bonus of all for Miss Bun and Miss Bee concerned one animal – the horse.

By chance, they had their television set installed at the start of the flat-racing season, and soon their greatest pleasure was to sit in front of the screen and watch every race of a televised meeting.

Partly this was because they happened to live in an area where horse-racing was almost a religion. Just on the other side of the hill across which the White Horse strode were some famous racing-stables, and the talk in the village pub (where the sisters did not go) or the shop (where they did) or between locals meeting in the street was always of form and racing certainties and red-hot tips and long-priced outsiders.

Partly they watched because Miss Bun and Miss Bee turned their race-viewing into a competition. They made their selections for each race and kept a careful score of points – 10 for a winner, 5 for a second place, 2 for a third. They took no notice of the tipsters' forecasts in the newspaper, nor of anything they might have heard in the village, but picked their horses for what they considered the most sensible reasons – liking the look of a particular animal, or its name, or the colours of its jockey's silks. No money was involved, but whichever sister scored the highest was allowed the sole use of the remote control for the rest of the day's viewing.

And the third reason for their pleasure in watching racing lay in the beauty of the animals themselves. To see a well-bred, perfectly turned-out racehorse parading around the paddock, or cantering to the start, or galloping at full stretch down the course, was sheer delight to Miss Bun and Miss Bee.

On this particular afternoon they were watching a meeting at Windsor, and by the end of the sixth and last race they had each had a very successful day at the races. Miss Bun had had three winners and three also-rans, but Miss Bee, though she had selected only two winners, had had two seconds and a third and only one horse out of the frame. She had therefore scored a total of 32 to Miss Bun's 30.

'Well done, Bee,' said Miss Bun. 'It's you to zap for the rest of the day.'

'You know, Bun,' said Miss Bee, 'I sometimes wish we were actually betting. That nag that I picked for the 3.30 – you know, the one with the pretty pink and green quartered colours – came in at 40 to 1. I'd have made a packet.'

'You'd soon have lost it all,' said Miss Bun. 'Betting's a mug's game.'

'I bet Lubber would have enjoyed watching racing,' Miss Bee said.

'We shall never know,' said Miss Bun.

'Never?'

'Well, it must be very long odds against his ever coming home again.'

'How long?'

'1,000 to 1 against, I should think.'

Chapter Ten

A BATTERING-RAM

As Katie approached Toddington Service Station, she saw the artic pulling out on to the motorway again. She dived and turned and flew alongside, to see three faces peering out from under the edge of the tarpaulin.

'You're goin' the wrong way!' she cried, but the roar of the engine drowned her voice.

As the artic picked up speed, the driver prepared to pass an old car that was doddering along in the slow lane. He glanced in his side-mirror and then began to pull out. As the tug angled a little to the trailer, he saw to his amazement that in addition to a load of meat for dogs, he was carrying two of them and a cat as well, while a racing pigeon flew alongside, its beak open for all the world as though it was talking to the other animals.

For a second or two he gazed spellbound, his eye off the road ahead, and veered over towards the fast lane. There was a furious hooting from a speeding car; the artic driver yanked back his steering-wheel, the tail of the trailer began to swing, and with a scream

of tortured tyres, J. Davidson's Nightly Trunk, Leeds to London, jack-knifed.

As the trailer swung, so it began to tip, and as it struck the guard-rails of the central reservation, the guy-ropes holding down the tarpaulin parted, the tarpaulin lifted like a flapping sail, and twenty cardboard boxes were catapulted over on to the other carriageway. Each box burst on impact, and in an instant the air was thick with the screech of brakes, the blaring of horns, and the cursing of drivers, as a thousand tins of Bonzo Top-Quality Dog Meat went rolling madly across the northbound M1.

So occupied were all the drivers in dodging the tins and each other that they hardly noticed two dogs and a cat go dashing across to the safety of the western verge, a pigeon flying above them.

Miraculously, no blood was spilt, and though the ensuing chaos resulted in much loss of time and temper and much damage to vehicles, the only other thing that was really hurt were the artic driver's feelings.

'Never 'ad an accident before,' he said to the police, when a patrol car arrived on the scene. 'Never in all me years of drivin'.'

The patrolmen looked at the jack-knifed artic and the small army of cars and vans and lorries, stationary now amidst a sea of tin cans.

'Well,' said one of them, 'you certainly made up for it today. Road's dry enough. You fall asleep or something?'

'Nah, guv,' said the driver. 'I just come out of Toddington Services.'

'Had a drink there, did you?'

'Tea, guv, just a cuppa, that's all.'

'How did it happen then?'

'Well,' said the driver, 'it was like this. I looks in me mirror, and there's a pigeon flying alongside and a Siamese cat and a brown-and-white dog and a red dog lookin' out over the edge of the trailer!'

'Fancy!' said the patrolman. 'And where was the pink elephant? Here, blow in this bag.'

The animals meanwhile had made themselves scarce. There was no getting through the motorway fence to open country beyond, but a quick recce by Katie had established that there was, not far away, a road-bridge that crossed the M1, so they hurried along the verge towards this.

Squintum was counting on the chance that there might be some way out for them at such a junction, only to be disappointed when they reached it. Then he noticed something, partly because he was the most observant, partly because he was lowest to the ground. An open concrete drain had been laid to run under the fence, whose wire netting had been extended to cover the area of the culvert and prevent wild animals like badgers or foxes from using it as an access to the motorway.

The drain was bone dry now, but many wet winters, Squintum could see, had rusted the wire that blocked it. He scratched at it and flakes fell from the metal.

'See this bit of wire here, Lubber?' he said.

Lubber looked at it. 'It's rusty,' he said.

'Exactly,' said Squintum, 'and therefore weakened. How do you fancy yourself as a ram?'

'A ram?' said Lubber. 'I don't see how . . .?'

'A battering-ram,' said Squintum. 'Charge at it. Bust your way through it. Worth a try, surely? You made a pretty good job of that door at the Dogs' Home, remember?'

'That was glass,' said Lubber.

'Oh well,' said Squintum off-handedly, turning away, 'if you're afraid of hurting yourself ... pity, it's our only chance of going on ... still, if you're going to be a scaredy-cat ...'

'Scaredy-cat, my paw!' shouted Lubber. 'Mind out of my way!' and he took a run and dived headfirst into the wire. Showers of rust fell off it, but it held firm, and Lubber was thrown backwards with a howl of pain and a bloody nose.

'Oh, poor Mr Lubber!' cooed Katie, perched on the rail of the bridge. ''Tis too strong for 'un, Mr Squintum.'

Squintum said nothing, but Colleen came forward and licked tenderly at Lubber's bleeding muzzle.

'It's not too strong for you, is it, Lubber?' she said softly. 'Not for you!'

Lubber's bushy tail, which had been clamped between his legs, began slowly to wave again, and he shook his hairy head to clear it and stood well back a second time.

'Once more unto the breach, dear friends!' he cried. 'Once more!' and with all his might he hurled himself recklessly forward and this time burst his way through.

'Faint heart,' said Squintum musingly, as he followed Colleen through the gap, 'ne'er won fair lady. Fly on then, Katie. Westward ho!'

Now they fell once again into the pattern of progress as before, Katie flying some way

84

ahead, and then waiting for the others to catch up.

Now she seemed much more confident of her direction. 'What do you think, Miss Colleen and gennulmen,' she said. 'I reckon it's comin' back to me,' and away she went again.

'What's coming back to her?' asked the Red Setter.

'Her sense of direction,' said Lubber. 'She lost it when a man nearly shot her. We're hoping that if she can find her home, she may find mine too.'

'In the thatched cottage, you mean?' said Colleen, for by now she had heard something of Lubber's story.

'In the little village,' said Squintum.

'Under the big hill,' said Lubber.

'With a White Horse on it!' they all chorused.

They pressed on through the fields bordering the road which had crossed the motorway. On the other side of the hedge Katie was waiting for them, sitting on top of a signpost, the better to be seen. The signpost pointed to a side road that ran up over the shoulder of a great sweep of downland. It said:

WHIPSNADE PARK ZOO

As they came near, the pigeon suddenly flew up high, and then commenced to treat them to a display of the aerobatic skills inherited from her distant tumbler ancestor, rolling and looping and diving and soaring and fluttering madly about the sky.

'Whatever's the matter with her?' said Colleen. 'Is she in trouble?'

'No,' said Squintum, 'it's high spirits. She's just doing it for a lark.'

'For a lark?' said Lubber. 'I don't see how . . .?'

'For fun,' said Squintum. 'She's as happy as a . . . Oh, forget it.'

Katie recovered herself at the last possible moment from a long twisting fall that seemed likely to be the death of her, and came to hover over them.

'Proper chalk country this be!' she cried down to them. 'You never know, we might be lucky soon!'

The others lay down in the grass, to have a rest and to see where Katie's next staging-point should be.

Suddenly they saw her swerve violently in flight, the kind of evasive action a pigeon might take if shot at or attacked by a bird of prey. But there was no sound of a gun or sight of a hawk, and almost immediately she turned and raced back to them, landing so fast beside them that she tipped over, beak first, as clumsily as if it had been her maiden flight.

'I saw it, I saw it!' she gabbled wildly. 'A girt big one!'

'A girt . . . I mean, a great big what?' said Squintum.

'A White Horse!'

Chapter Eleven

A NICE BRIGHT
RED COAT

'A White Horse?' barked Lubber. 'My White Horse?'

'More'n likely, Mr Lubber,' said Katie. 'It's on a big hill all right, on the side of the downs opposite, a hugeous girt thing it is. If you get high enough, you'll be able to see it too. Go on up that slope ahead.'

'Come on, Colleen!' shouted Lubber, and the two dogs raced off. One was still not much more than a puppy and the other was a great big puppy at heart, and they gambolled wildly, barking with excitement and chasing one another as they ran up the rising ground.

Squintum followed at his own pace. A White Horse there might be, but he remembered Katie's words as they had talked together at the fringe of that copse, many miles to the north.

'Oh, there's several of them about,' she had said.

We must hope, he thought as he padded up the rise behind the dogs, that it is not only a

White Horse but the right horse, for to find his home means everything to Lubber. As for me, it does not signify. I shall be glad for his sake if we succeed, very glad, and I feel sure that Colleen will be welcomed too, but for myself, I shall wait and see. Lubber's old ladies may not be cat-loving people, and I am none too sure that I am a people-loving cat. If we do not suit, it will not be the end of the world.

At the top of the rise he caught up with the rest of the party. Lubber and Colleen sat with their backs to a post-and-rail fence on which Katie perched, and all three stared southward, where, from this added height, they could now clearly see the enormous shape on the shoulder of the downs opposite them.

'There 'tis,' said Katie with satisfaction. 'Funny-lookin' old horse, but there 'tis.'

'That's not my White Horse,' said Lubber dolefully. 'It doesn't look anything like it.'

'It doesn't look much like a horse at all to me,' said Colleen.

The Siamese looked and gave a yowl of amusement. For him, there was no mistaking the identity of that huge figure cut in the chalk, with its massive maned head and powerful body and long tufted tail. It was a picture of the noblest of his family, the King of Beasts.

'It's not a horse!' he said. 'It's a lion!'

'Oh dear!' said Katie in a melancholy voice. 'Oh, I'm sorry, Mr Lubber, raisin' your hopes like that.'

Lubber sighed. 'That's all right, Katie,' he said.

'Katie will find you a white horse sooner or later, I'm sure,' said Colleen comfortingly. 'Won't you, Katie?'

'I hope so, miss,' said Katie. 'I'll try my best, I will.'

'Well spoken, Katie,' said Squintum. 'You can't say fairer than that.'

Morale among the troops was at a low ebb, he saw, and he set himself to distract them. He knew, like another, more famous little general before him, that an army marches on its stomach, and he felt sure that a good feed and a rest would work wonders.

'Time we all had some grub,' he said. 'We'll meet back here later. No problem for you, is it, Katie?'

'Oh no, Mr Squintum, sir,' said Katie. 'Not at harvest-time. The combines is out workin', I did see, but there's corn a-plenty about,' and off she flew.

'Right,' said Squintum, 'I fancy a few field-mice for starters,' and he made to move off.

'Hey, wait a minute!' called Lubber. 'What about us? What are we supposed to do for food?'

'Use your eyes,' said Squintum over his shoulder. 'Look at that big meadow just below you,' and away he went.

'Look at a meadow?' said Lubber. 'What does he expect us to do – eat grass like a cow?'

Colleen did not answer. She stood, alert and tense, plumy red tail outstretched, her muzzle pointing down the slope beyond, the picture of vigilance.

'What is it?' said Lubber, and then he saw what she was looking at.

At the far end of the field were a score or more rabbits, grazing, hopping about in the sunshine, chasing one another in play or aggression, or sitting up and grooming.

An experienced dog like a lurcher would have slipped down the outside of the hedge, keeping out of sight, till he was near enough. But Lubber and Colleen were beginners both in the art of rabbit-catching, and they simply took off and charged down the meadow. By the time they reached the far end, there wasn't a rabbit to be seen.

'Little devils!' said Lubber. 'They were too quick for us,' but as the two dogs made their way back up the hill, they almost trod on an outlying rabbit that had remained squatting in a tussock of grass.

Colleen was fast, much faster than Lubber, but the rabbit would have been too quick for her on her own. Indeed, it had almost reached the safety of the hedge when Lubber, galloping madly, cut it off, and it jinked and met Colleen and jinked again and met its death.

When they had eaten it, they began to search the neighbouring fields, and as they hunted together, so their technique improved. There were no more blind charges, but instead they worked stealthily, to come between the rabbits and their hedgerow burrows and force them out into the open. Here, the speedy Colleen would course them, and Lubber, running wide on her flank, would hope to turn them.

The rabbits, they soon found, hadn't the brains to learn from their escapes, and as the two dogs made their rounds, they found that those who had been chased not half an hour before had forgotten all about it and had popped out again. Most escaped, of course, but by evening they had killed three more, plump young ones at that, and their bellies were full.

Indeed, as the party pressed on, rabbits were the staple food of the dogs, expert enough now to provide the odd one for Squintum too as a change from mice and voles. Water was no problem, for if they did not come upon a stream, there were always cattle-troughs to drink from, and the regular foot-slogging, day in, day out, in the fine summer weather, kept them as fit as fleas.

Lubber, Squintum saw, had lost all his tub-
biness, and though he liked his night's sleep
he had no chance to laze by day, for Squintum
kept them on the march.

Sometimes, when the going was easy, they
covered ten miles in a day, but it might be no
more than three or four where there were
towns to be avoided or railway tracks to be
crossed or other such hazards. And always
the route hugged the northern edge of the
great escarpment of chalk that runs from
Bedfordshire to Buckinghamshire to Berk-
shire and so to the Wiltshire downs.

'So long as I do stick close to the chalk,'
said Katie. 'We can't go wrong. Whether 'tis
pictures of horses or lions or whatever,
they're all made of the chalk.'

So the weeks passed, quickly it seemed to the
travellers, so happy were they in one another's company, and harvest was over
(though there was still plenty of food for the
pigeon in the stubbles), and the leaves began
to change colour as September drew on.

Now they found themselves on the edges of
a great valley, perhaps ten miles wide and as
many as twenty or more miles long. They did
not of course know its name, though it might
have gladdened their hearts if they had, for
this was the Vale of the White Horse.

They woke one autumn morning in a little
wood at the southern side of this valley, and
were about to set out on the day's march,

when an unusual sound came to their ears. A sharp clear sound it was, all the more so in the quiet of a day that had dawned crisp and still. It was the rooty-toot of a huntsman's horn.

Three of them had never heard such a thing before, but Lubber had, once, as a puppy, when the local hunt had met in his village and, moving off to draw, had passed right by the gate of Horseview Cottage.

Instantly he remembered the sound, and the sight of the man who had carried the horn, a big red-faced, scarlet-coated man on a big black horse. How he had whined and struggled in the arms of Miss Bun and Miss Bee to be allowed to join the pack as hounds swung up the lane, huntsman and whippers-in following the Master, and behind, the field of riders, some in scarlet coats, some in black, some in rat-catcher; men, women and children, mounted on horses of every colour, that varied in size from great rawboned hunters to roly-poly ponies.

Now the horn sounded again, nearer.

'What is it?' asked Squintum.

'It's the foxhounds,' said Lubber, 'out cubbing.'

'Cubbing?' said Colleen.

'Cub-hunting,' said Lubber, proud of his knowledge for once. 'They don't begin proper hunting till October, but once the harvest is off, cubbing starts. It's partly to cut down the number of this season's fox-cubs, and partly to enter young hounds that have never hunted before. They learn from the older ones, you see, and they get a taste of blood.'

'Hm,' said Squintum. 'These hounds . . . they only kill foxes, eh?'

'Oh yes,' said Lubber confidently. 'That's why they're called foxhounds.'

At that minute, they heard a man's voice, quite close, it seemed.

'Leu in! Leu in!' said the voice, and then they heard a crackle of sticks and the whimper of a hound, nearer still.

'Beggin' your pardon, Miss Colleen, gennulmen,' said Katie, 'but I'd be happier aloft,' and she flew up into the crown of a great chestnut tree.

'Me, too,' said Squintum, and he ran up its trunk and settled himself on a branch.

'You're confident,' he called down to Lubber, 'that they only kill foxes? You're sure about that, I hope?'

Whatever answer Lubber made was drowned in a sudden great crash of noise as the pack picked up the scent, and twenty couple gave tongue with one mighty voice. Such was the volume of sound among the trees that it was hard to tell exactly what direction it came from, but one thing was sure. It was very close.

Next moment there was a rustle in the bushes, and out came a fox. This was no cub but an old grey-muzzled dog fox, and he swerved at the sight of Lubber and Colleen, and snarled at them as he sped past.

'There's a nice bright red coat your girl-friend's got!' he said to Lubber out of the corner of his mouth. 'Mind she doesn't get mistaken for something else!'

Chapter Twelve

DREAMS

At that precise moment, Miss Bun and Miss Bee's old tin alarm clock went off. It stood, as always, on the table between their beds, and it went off, as always, at precisely 6.45 a.m.

The sisters' morning routine always reversed the previous night's privilege: that is to say, whichever sister had lost the evening game and thus come to bed last was allowed to remain in comfort, while the other went down to make tea and bring it up on a tray. In fact, neither minded doing this, as it meant two extra rides on the chair-lift.

It was Miss Bun who had triumphed at last night's Beggar My Neighbour, so it was she who got out of bed, picked up her walking-stick, and, leaning on it, drew back the curtains.

As always happened – whichever sister it was – the first comment referred to the great animal that strode for ever across the slope opposite, yet never made a yard of progress. They liked to imagine that the White Horse was affected by each day's weather. If it was bad – wet or cold – they fancied that he hung his head a little, sad and downcast at being left up on the down to face alone the worst of the elements. But if the weather was good, he seemed jaunty, they thought, his step brisker, his ears cocked a fraction more. And on the kind of morning that promised a perfectly beautiful day, Miss Bun and Miss Bee were almost certain that there was a twinkle in the single eye of the White Horse.

'How does he look, Bun?' asked Miss Bee.

'Pretty good,' said Miss Bun. 'It's going to be quite nice, I should say. I'll go and make the tea.'

She had come back, riding happily up on the chair-lift with a tray balanced on her knees (Earl Grey for herself, Lapsang Souchong for Miss Bee), and they were sitting up in bed, cup and saucer in hand, when Miss Bee said, 'Do you know, Bun, I was so glad when the alarm went off.'

'Glad? Why?'

'Because I was having a horrid dream.'

'What was it about?'

'I don't really know. It was in a wood, and suddenly there was a terrible noise and the wood was full of dogs, dozens of big dogs. And something awful was going to happen, I felt sure.'

'How odd, Bee,' said Miss Bun. 'I had a dream about a dog too. Not a nightmare like yours though. I just dreamt that I rode downstairs to make the tea and there was Lubber asleep in his basket under the kitchen table. It was so real that just now I half expected to see him there.'

Miss Bee took a sip of her Lapsang.

'That basket must never be put away, don't you agree, Bun?' she said.

'Never,' said Miss Bun, finishing off her Earl Grey. 'Not if I live to be a hundred.'

'I'd rather you said a hundred and two,' said Miss Bee.

'Why?'

'Because then I should have got to a hundred as well.'

'Fat chance we've got!' said Miss Bun.

'You never know your luck,' said Miss Bee.

Chapter Thirteen

BACKED LIKE
A WEASEL

Luck was running out fast for the second fox to appear. No sooner had the old greymuzzle vanished from sight than the cub came dashing madly along, the pack driving through the trees behind it. The leading hounds were not a dozen yards behind its brush as it ran beneath the chestnut tree, in whose branches Katie and Squintum were perched.

The cub suddenly caught sight of Lubber and Colleen still standing irresolute, and it checked, hesitated, swerved off to one side, and was buried in a growling, snarling, wrenching tide.

'Tear 'im and eat 'im!' yelled the huntsman, thundering up, and Colleen fled in horror.

Just as he had done once before, 'Run for it!' squawled Squintum to Lubber at the top of his awful voice. 'Follow her! Or else they'll kill you!'

Had all the pack been busy at the worry, the two dogs might have made their escape without trouble; but now, while Lubber still dithered, half a dozen young hounds appeared, running wide and pursued by an angry whipper-in. Carried away by the thrill of this their first hunt, they had been chasing anything they could see.

''Ware rabbit!' yelled the whipper-in, and 'Get away back to 'im!' but before he could catch up with them, they caught sight of a fleeing red shape and away they went after Colleen.

From his grandstand seat, Squintum had a perfect view of what followed. He saw Colleen come suddenly upon another horseman who shouted at her, so that, confused and panicky now, she changed direction, almost towards her pursuers.

He saw the six young hounds closing in on her.

He saw the whipper-in dodging among the trees, whip cracking.

And finally he saw Lubber, galloping to the rescue.

'I'm coming, Colleen!' he roared, and he ran blindly at the foxhounds.

Wild with excitement, they had tumbled the Red Setter over and the foremost of them was going for her throat, when a hairy brown-and-white thunderbolt hit him squarely in the ribs and knocked him flying.

For a moment the rioting hounds hesitated, but their blood was up and they were six to one, and now they flung themselves on Lubber.

100

Bravely he fought them, Squintum saw, fastening his teeth in a foreleg here and a pad there, and roaring his defiance, but it might have gone hard with him had not help arrived in time.

'Garn leave it!' cried the whipper-in. 'Gaaaarn leave it, willya!' and the lash of his whip flicked here and there like a striking snake, till the three couple of hounds ran, yelping like the puppies they had but recently been, back to rejoin the pack. Two of them, Squintum saw, were limping badly.

'Damned dogs!' swore the whipper-in, as he pulled his horse round to follow.

He looked angrily at the trembling Colleen and the panting, dishevelled Lubber, and his whip cracked above their heads like a pistol shot.

'Damned people walking their damned dogs in the countryside!' he said. 'They've got no right!' and away he went.

'Oh, Lubber!' said Colleen. 'You saved my life!'

She licked at one of his ears which was badly ripped.

'My hero!' she said.

'Oh, I say, Colleen!' said Lubber in an embarrassed voice, but he felt a glow of pleasure that more than outweighed the pain of the bites he had received.

They waited until their ears and noses told them that the hunt had moved on to draw another wood, and then they made their way back to the chestnut tree.

Katie, who had seen nothing from her perch in the crown, came fluttering down. 'What a racket they make, they fox-dogs,' she said. 'I don't want to come across them no more if that's what they doos.'

Squintum, who had seen everything, came down the trunk. 'Be good enough to see which way they've gone, would you, Katie?' he said, and when the pigeon had flown away, he said, 'What damage?'

'I'm all right,' said Colleen. 'They knocked me over, but Lubber came up before they could hurt me. He saved my life!'

'A hero,' said Squintum gravely.

'Oh, I say, Squintum!' said Lubber.

'Are you hurt?'

'Not really,' said Lubber. 'It's useful, having

a lot of hair. Just a scratch on one ear, that's all.'

Squintum inspected it. 'A scratch?' he said. 'It's nearly torn in half. You'll carry the mark of that to your dying day.'

Colleen shivered. 'Oh don't, Squintum!' she said. 'Let's get out of this horrible place, can't we?'

As if in answer, they heard Katie's voice above.

'All clear!' she called. 'They're huntin' another fox, goin' east, away from us.'

They made ten miles that day, travelling as fast as the slowest member of the party, Squintum, could manage, anxious to put red coats and thundering horses and the fearful music of hounds far behind them.

As night fell, the Siamese and the two dogs came to the end of their final stage to see Katie sitting, as she often did, on top of a roadside signpost. It was a finger-post really, with just one arm that said:

KINGSTON LISLE

They spent that night in the shelter of a great sandy bank that ran beneath a long row of beech trees. Katie went to roost in one of these, and the others, tired out by travel and the drama of the day, curled up under the bank and slept like logs. Even Squintum, creature of the night, slept deeply, though later in the small hours he was conscious of hearing some strange noises, gruntings and chatterings, and of smelling an unfamiliar smell.

At dawn, he discovered the origin of both sound and scent.

Poking out of a large hole, not far away in the bank, was a broad grey head marked with two narrow black stripes and, between them, a wide white stripe.

'Wake up!' hissed Squintum to the dogs.

'What is it?' said Colleen nervously. 'Is it dangerous?'

'I don't know,' said Squintum. He hissed angrily at Lubber, still in the land of dreams.

'Wake up!' he said again.

'Eh? What's the matter?' said Lubber, yawning hugely. He got to his feet and stretched.

'Ouch!' he said. 'I'm sore all over.'

'You'll be sorer in a minute if you don't answer my question,' said Squintum. 'What is that animal?'

Lubber peered from under his bushy eyebrows at the head in the hole. 'Oh, I saw one of those once,' he said. 'Got run over, just outside our cottage. My old ladies were ever so upset about it, you should have heard them.'

'Well, what is it?' said Colleen.

'It's a badger.'

At the sound of its name, the animal came further out, so that they all could now clearly see its low broad body and powerful, strong-clawed feet and stumpy tail. It turned its striped head and called down the hole. 'Remain within, my dear, I prithee,' said the boar badger, 'and I beg you will not allow the children out. I will send these intruders about their business.'

The badger's tones were deep and cultured, and at the sound of his voice, with its curiously old-fashioned delivery, Squintum perceived immediately that here was no country bumpkin, but a gentleman of breeding, like himself. 'I do assure you, sir,' he said silkily, 'that we have no wish to intrude and must apologize for so doing.'

'What do ye here?' grunted the badger.

'We are merely passing through. We are travellers.'

'Whence come ye?'

'Well, in strict point of fact,' said Squintum, 'I come from Siam and my young friend here from Ireland.'

The badger pointed his snout at Lubber.

'And thou?' he said. 'Where is thy home?'

Lubber hesitated, for this was what he did not truly know, but Squintum cut in quickly.

'My hairy friend,' he said, 'is temporarily lost, and we are trying to return him to his owners. We should be most grateful if you could assist us with your local knowledge. Have you lived long in these parts?'

The boar badger seemed mollified by Squintum's civil manner, and he answered in a voice that was less curt and gruff.

'Verily,' he said, 'I have dwelt here all my

life, cub and boar, and my father before me likewise, and his father, and his father, and so back through the centuries. Always there have been badgers here in this set, even unto the times when ancient men cut the shape of the great beast in the hillside behind us.'

'The ... shape ... of ... the ... great ... beast?' said Squintum slowly. 'What beast?'

'Why, the White Horse,' said the boar. 'Dost thou not know that thou art in the Vale of the White Horse?'

'D'you hear that?' barked Lubber excitedly. 'Colleen, Squintum, d'you hear that? Katie, where are you, come along, we're there, we've found it, we're nearly home!' and he dashed off over the top of the bank with Colleen following, and Katie flying after.

'I must apologize for my friend's exuberance, sir,' said Squintum, 'but a white horse is the key that we seek. He lives opposite it. Many thanks for your help,' and off he went after the others.

'Good fortune attend thee,' called the boar badger after him, 'but take heed, this Horse is like none other that I ever saw. Methinks it is like a weasel. It is backed like a weasel.'

Oh no, thought Squintum as he ran, not another disappointment for poor Lubber, but when he caught up with the rest he could see straightaway how dejected the big dog looked. He hung his head, while Colleen licked at his ripped ear.

Squintum looked across at the distant downs, and there was another chalk figure, a figure of the strangest shape. It was long, almost four hundred feet in length, and thin. One hindleg and one foreleg were detached from the snake-like body, and at the end of the curved neck was a head with a curious beaked muzzle. To the ancient men who had designed it, it was their idea of a horse, but to Squintum it looked like nothing so much as the skinniest of alley-cats slinking away over the crest of the hill. He could think of nothing to say, but Katie summed it up.

'Backed the wrong horse again, haven't we?' she said.

Chapter Fourteen

SNAP!

'Ah well, third time lucky,' said Squintum drily. 'Come on, let's find something to eat, we'll feel better then.'

In fact, as though to make up for the disappointment, they had a couple of bits of good fortune.

First of all, the dogs found a leveret, or young hare, that was lying so still and scentless in its form in the middle of a pasture that Lubber almost trod on it, and Colleen grabbed it before it could get into its stride.

Then, passing through a spinney, they came upon a fine cock pheasant, a runner, one wing having been broken by a sportsman's shot, and run though he did, they ran faster.

On the following day, they came to another motorway that ran east and west.

'It's the one I was tellin' you about, Mr Squintum,' said Katie when she came back to report it. 'We're on the right track, that's for sure.'

'The right track for your home maybe,' said

Lubber heavily, 'but what about mine?'

'We'll find yours,' said Colleen. 'We've only got to find the right White Horse and we're there. Katie's got to find her loft, that's much harder.'

'It is now,' said Katie. 'Time was when you could have thrown me up anywhere in England and I'd have gone for home straight as a die. Used to come down from Lunnon, following this very motorway and then turn off ... somewhere ... only now I can't remember where. I know we're goin' roughly right, but I'm not exactly sure of the way. From here on 'tis a matter of luck, I reckon. I'll tell you somethin' though – I don't care all that much whether I find my loft or no. I just like bein' with you gennulmen and Miss Colleen! I don't think I want to go racin' any more – I'm not so young as I was. What do you think, Mr Lubber, do you think your old ladies might like a pigeon for a pet?'

'I'm sure they would, Katie,' said Lubber. 'I'm sure they'll welcome all of us. If only we can find them.'

'We're not going to find them by sitting here chattering,' said Squintum sharply. 'Have a look for a road-bridge across the motorway, Katie. We'll have to cross in the dark.'

That evening the pigeon led them close to the M4 and they lay up with the roar of the traffic in their ears. They crossed in the small hours, over a bridge signposted:

and seeing the loom of a nearby town, said farewell to the Vale of the White Horse and struck up on to the downs.

They slept through the morning, but for none of them, not even for Lubber, was it a deep sleep. Thus far the weather had been perfect for their odyssey, but summer was long past now and the wind had gone round into the east, blowing cold and strong across the high downlands.

Squintum in particular thought longingly of a cosy fireside. His pads were sore from travelling, and he was more than usually sharp-tongued.

At midday they sought shelter in a beech-hanger and rested awhile. Then they split up to find the day's food.

Katie flew off to find stubbles as yet un-ploughed, the dogs went rabbiting and Squintum set out on mouse patrol.

He was out of temper, with the weather, with his sore feet, with the whole business that he had let himself in for. How much longer must they keep on, day in, day out, with winter coming and no guarantee that they would ever find this thatched cottage in this little village under this big hill with this confounded White Horse on it. Yet there was no going back, they could only keep on.

'Damnation upon all white horses!' spat Squintum, as he padded hastily and angrily along a tunnel-like runway in the under-growth.

Suddenly there was a sharp metallic 'snap', and Squintum felt an agonizing pain in one hindfoot, a pain so sudden and searing and shocking that he gave a loud shrill scream.

Maybe if he had been less angry, he would have seen or smelt the gin-trap set in the centre of the runway under a scatter of leaves. But then again, if his ill-temper had not made him stride out in haste, he might have put a foot squarely on the pan of the trap and been caught now, firmly and finally, by the toothed steel jaws.

As it was, he had almost cleared it, by chance leaping over it and only springing it at the last instant with a trailing hindfoot, two of whose toes were held now in a vice-like grip.

Gone in a flash was all Squintum's self-possession, all his worldly-wisdom, all his powers of leadership and decision. He was nothing but a terrified wild beast, and he scrabbled madly with his three good feet to get free of the dreadful thing that had him in its power.

But the gin-trap was fixed with a strong strand of wire to a stout peg driven well into the ground, precisely to prevent the escape of whatever creature its jaws might hold, for trappers do not discriminate when they set their vile, unlawful machines.

Squintum was a prisoner, destined first for suffering and then for death. Lubber and

Colleen came rushing at the sound of his first piercing yowls, arriving to find him lying stretched upon his side, gasping for breath. The gaze in his blue eyes seemed to cross even more than usual as he looked dully up at them, and he could only mew 'Help me! Help me!' in the voice of a hurt kitten.

All was plain to the two dogs. They saw the peg that held the wire that held the gin that held the crushed and bleeding toes. All this they saw, but not what they could possibly do to save the Siamese.

Then they heard a sound, not far off. It was a crackling in the bushes, and then they caught the scent of the man who, walking his trap-line, had heard the screams and was coming to investigate.

Squintum scented him too and knew, through his pain, that if he could not get free, this was the end, however many lives he might have in credit.

A man who set illegal gins, for rabbit or hare, for weasel or stoat, for fox or badger, a man who cared not what was caught, would have only one response to a trapped cat. He would smash in its skull with a stick.

With all the strength that fear lent him, Squintum made one final effort. He drew back a little, and then he hurled himself desperately forward.

When the trapper arrived at the spot a couple of minutes later, all that remained in the bloodstained jaws of the gin were two dark brown, sharp-clawed toes.

Chapter Fifteen

NEARLY HOME

Ever since Squintum had screeched that first order at him, in the vet's surgery in the Dogs' Home, Lubber had been accustomed to obeying the Siamese cat. Squintum was the leader, and it was the duty of the rest of them to abide by his decisions.

How different things were now.

Lubber, bringing up the rear, watched his friend anxiously as the three of them hurried through the beech-hanger as fast as they could; as fast, that is, as Squintum could limp. A little trail of blood-drops marked his progress.

They had gone perhaps half a mile when Squintum suddenly stopped and lay down. He was panting, with exertion, with pain and with shock.

Lubber looked back. There was no sign of the man following them yet, but he might, and the further they went from this place of traps, the better.

'Come on, Squintum, old chap,' he said. 'We must get on.'

'Can't!' whined Squintum, still in a kitten's voice. 'My foot hurts!'

'What shall we do?' said Colleen, but she said it not to the Siamese, as always before, but to Lubber. 'Lubber, what shall we do?'

Suddenly, for the first time in his life, Lubber felt masterful.

'I'll tell you what we'll do,' he said.

He looked ahead to the crest of a high hill that rose in front of them.

'Colleen,' he said, 'you make for the top of that hill and wait for us there. Keep an eye out for Katie, she'll probably spot you anyway, and if you can pick up a rabbit on the way, so much the better. Go on, off you go.'

'Yes, Lubber,' said Colleen obediently, and away she went.

'And as for you,' said Lubber to Squintum, 'on your feet, or three of them anyway, and get moving!'

He forced himself to speak in a brutal way, fearing that the cat was giving up, and when the only reply was another 'Can't!', he said, 'Yes, you can and you will. Just thank your lucky stars you've got plenty of lives left yet, and get up and go, or I'll bite you, d'you hear me?'

When at last they reached the distant hilltop, Colleen was waiting with a rabbit in her jaws. Katie was perched on a nearby bush. She hopped down when she saw the limping cat and waddled over to him.

'Oh my heavens, Mr Squintum, sir!' she cried. 'Whatever's happened? Why, there's only two toes left on that foot!'

Squintum made no answer but only lay and licked at his wounds. The bleeding had stopped, Lubber could see, but he saw also that the patient would need rest, and good feeding, and time for healing, and protection against other possible enemies.

Lubber drew the Setter and the racing pigeon to one side.

'Listen to me,' he said. 'We're staying put for as long as it takes him to recover, understand? From up here we can see anyone coming, and by the look of things, there's no shortage of rabbits around. That's your job, Colleen, on your own now, because I'm staying here on guard. You'll have to provide for the three of us. Can you manage?'

'Oh yes,' said Colleen confidently. She too seemed to have drawn strength from Squintum's weakness. 'There are quite a few young ones still about,' she said, 'without as much sense or speed as the adults. I'll keep you supplied, don't worry.'

'Right,' said Lubber. 'Now, Katie, this delay gives you the perfect chance to make a really detailed survey of the area. We're on the highest point for miles around, and if you fly out on a straight course in a slightly different direction each day, you'll have every chance of finding the White Horse.'

'Yes, Mr Lubber, sir,' said Katie respectfully.

'I'll find it, see if I don't.'

In fact, once Squintum was properly rested and the shock of his experience had faded, his recovery was swift. Fit and hard, with the natural resilience of his kind, and well fed now by Colleen who had hunted tirelessly and successfully, he was soon something like his old self again. To be sure, the loss of his toes was to leave him with a permanent slight limp, but the wound healed swiftly and well, and before a week was up he told Lubber he was fit to travel.

As an added bonus the weather, which had threatened to be wintry, changed completely, and it seemed now, in mid-October, that they were to be favoured with that lovely late fine spell that humans call St Luke's Little Summer.

Only Katie, methodically flying out on a different radius each day, had as yet nothing to report. But Lubber was anxious to move on.

Added to his new-found authority was a strong feeling, which he had never had before, that the end of their quest was not so very far away; and one morning before dawn he led Squintum and Colleen south, on a line of his own choosing.

On their right or western side ran a main road, and, moving parallel to this over the downs, they came shortly upon the strangest of places.

Long before they reached them they could see the standing stones, huge slabs of rock, maybe thirty of them in all, set upright in the turf in two concentric circles.

'Whatever are those?' asked Colleen as they approached.

'Stones,' said Lubber laconically.

'But why? . . . How did they get to be like that? . . . Who put them there?' she said. 'Squintum, do you know?'

Squintum prowled among the standing stones, making an odd singsong yarring in his throat. He did not know the reason for these great strange objects, or for the many long barrows that they had passed, or for the enormous bee-hive-shaped hump that he could now see not far ahead of them. But he felt instinctively that these were mystical magical places, places of long-dead folk.

'I don't know what they are,' he said, 'but there is something in me that fears them.'

'Afraid of a stone?' said Lubber. 'What rubbish!'

'I don't know *why* they are there, either,' said Squintum.

'I do,' said Lubber, and he walked up to the largest one and cocked his leg on it.

At that moment they saw Katie coming in fast from the west. She did not make her customary circuit before landing, but dropped straight down and pitched on top of the newly christened standing stone. She bobbed backwards and forwards, not in her usual respectful manner, but out of excitement. Yet she did not speak.

Then they saw why. She had something in her beak – a white object about the size of a sugar lump – and now she dropped it in front of them and said in a triumphant voice, 'What do you think of that then?'

'It's a lump of chalk,' said Lubber, sniffing at it.

'You're right,' said Katie. 'But where did I get it?'

'Where *did* you get it?'

'Off a horse.'

'Off a horse?' said Lubber. 'I don't see how ... oh ... oh yes, I do! You've found it, Katie! You've found the White Horse! Was it on a big hill?'

'So it was.'

'Was there a little village under the hill?' asked Colleen.

'So there was.'

'Was there a thatched cottage in the village?' asked Squintum.

'You're right,' said Katie, 'and what's more, I flew down there to have a proper look, and there was two old ladies walkin' in the garden of that cottage, arm in arm they were, and each of 'em had a walkin'-stick in her other hand. What do you think of that then?'

'Well, Lubber,' said Squintum, 'it looks as though you're nearly home.'

'We're nearly home, you mean,' said Lubber. 'How far is it, Katie?'

''Bout four mile.'

'Fly on then. Lead us on.'

Katie led them first over the main road that they had been skirting. There was hardly any traffic and they slipped across unseen. It was the same with a second main road, running east and west this time, and then they found themselves entering a valley whose flat bed was carpeted with long stretches of firm, close turf. Here, though they did not know it, were the gallops of a racing stables, and they were half-way along the valley when they heard a distant rumble of hooves. They watched from cover as the long string of racehorses, their glossy coats gleaming in the early sunshine, went galloping by in single file. Black and brown, chestnut and bay, they thundered past, the hunched men on their backs seeming hardly larger than monkeys.

'Every colour but the one we want,' said Lubber to Katie when next they caught up with her.

'Not long now, Mr Lubber,' she said. 'See that round clump of trees on the skyline yonder? Meet me up there. It's just beyond.'

Lubber's instinct was to rush madly after her, but he knew too well how much he owed to Squintum, and he forced himself to match his pace to the cat's limp.

The clump was almost silent when they reached it, for it was late in the year for bird-song, and the only sounds as they made their way under the trees were the gentle noise of the wind in their leaves and the contented cooing of 82/708/KT, perched somewhere high above.

Before them, as they emerged on the far side, the northern slope fell steeply away, and staring down it they saw, almost at their feet, the outline of yet another great figure cut in the chalk.

'Is it?' cried Colleen eagerly. 'Is it your horse, Lubber?'

'I don't recognize it,' said Lubber slowly. 'Its legs are sticking up. It seems to be lying on its back.'

Squintum looked down at it and then further down, to the little village that lay under the hill, and saw there, a short way along a lane, the thatched roof of a cottage.

the sisters kept an old pair of binoculars, which occasionally they used to identify birds in the garden. Now Miss Bun, roused by the urgency in her sister's voice, levered herself out of bed and made her way to the window, carrying the glasses. She propped herself against her sister and, raising them to her eyes, aimed them at the distant Horse and began to adjust the focus.

Then she gave a little scream.

Then she handed them to Miss Bee.

Then Miss Bee gave a little scream too.

'It couldn't be, could it, Bun?' she cried.

'It could,' said Miss Bun. 'Quick, let's get dressed.'

'But the tea . . .?'

'Oh, blow the tea! You shall ride down first anyway.'

Twenty minutes later, they stood arm in arm propped on their sticks, at the gate of Horse-view Cottage, and gazed up the lane.

And presently down the lane came a large hairy mongrel, white with brown patches, with a long bushy tail and floppy ears, one of them badly torn.

'Lubber!' cried Miss Bun and Miss Bee with one joyous voice, and they threw wide the gate.

So busy were they with greeting him and patting him and stroking him and calling him every endearment under the sun, that at first they did not notice that he was not alone. Waiting politely in the lane were two other animals, a beautiful young Red Setter bitch and an elegant Siamese cat.

'Oh look, Bun!' said Miss Bee. 'He's brought some friends!'

'We must invite them in,' said Miss Bun, and they both cried, 'Come in! Come in, do!'

The sisters watched spellbound as Lubber, tail gently wagging, walked slowly up the garden path, followed by the others. The cat, they noticed, was lame. Like me, each thought.

Then the three animals stopped as if by mutual agreement and stood in a row on the lawn, and looked up into the clear sky. And out of it there came tumbling a racing pigeon with long, slaty-blue, tapering wings; a pigeon that looped and rolled and twisted above the cottage and finally swooped down to land at the feet of Miss Bun and Miss Bee. It bobbed respectfully at them, and then began to strut about the lawn on its pink legs, on one of which, the sisters could see, was a blue ring stamped with a number.

Miss Bun and Miss Bee looked at Lubber, standing masterfully between the Red Setter and the Siamese cat, while the racing pigeon cooed before them. Then they looked at one another, and shook their heads, and smiled.

'Good job we kept the dog-basket, Bee,' said Miss Bun.

'We shall have to get a second one.'

'And a cat-basket.'

'And a pigeon-cote.'

'Make the tea, Bee,' said Miss Bun. 'It's your turn.'

That evening Lubber and Squintum walked round the garden together. They, and Colleen, had had a delicious meal. Miss Bun was grooming all the burs and brambles from the Setter's red coat, and Miss Bee was feeding Katie with little bits of Garibaldi biscuit.

'Shall you stay, Squintum?' said Lubber.

'I might,' said Squintum.

'Worth a try, surely?' said Lubber, in an imitation of his friend's nasal voice, and the Siamese purred and rubbed himself against the big dog's hairy legs.

'I'll give it six months,' he said.

Chapter Seventeen

HAPPY ENDING

Six months later, on a lovely morning in mid-April, Miss Bun and Miss Bee sat on a seat by the lawn at Horseview Cottage. Squintum was curled lazily between them, and Katie perched on the back of the seat, bubbling and cooing.

In front of them all, Lubber and Colleen lay

on the grass, resting their chins on the edge of a large wicker dog-basket, inside which lay a great many fat little creatures. Some of them were fast asleep, some twitched and squeaked softly in their dreams. Some of them were red, and some were white with brown patches. Some of them were silky, and some of them were already rather hairy.

But on one thing there was general agreement.

These were the most beautiful puppies ever born.

Everybody watched, happy as could be, in the spring sunshine, under the White Horse.